Jewelry Ca

Sage Gardens Cozy Mystery Series

Cindy Bell

Copyright © 2015 Cindy Bell
All rights reserved.

All rights reserved. No part of this publication may be reproduced or transmitted in any form or by any means, electronic or mechanical, including photocopy, recording, or any information storage or retrieval system, without permission in writing from the publisher.

This is a work of fiction. The characters, incidents and locations portrayed in this book and the names herein are fictitious. Any similarity to or identification with the locations, names, characters or history of any person, product or entity is entirely coincidental and unintentional.

All trademarks and brands referred to in this book are for illustrative purposes only, are the property of their respective owners and not affiliated with this publication in any way. Any trademarks are being used without permission, and the publication of the trademark is not authorized by, associated with or sponsored by the trademark owner.

ISBN-13: 978-1519733078

ISBN-10: 1519733070

Table of Contents

Chapter One 1

Chapter Two 18

Chapter Three 27

Chapter Four 41

Chapter Five 50

Chapter Six 64

Chapter Seven 87

Chapter Eight 106

Chapter Nine 128

Chapter Ten.. 150

Chapter Eleven 161

Chapter Twelve... 177

Chapter Thirteen 190

Chapter Fourteen 206

Chapter Fifteen 227

Chapter Sixteen 241

Chapter Seventeen... 255

Chapter One

Samantha tried to grab the muffin out of the muffin pan. It was still so hot that it burnt the tips of her fingers.

"Ouch!" She sighed as the muffin fell back into the pan. With a fork and knife combination she managed to get the muffin out of the pan and into the basket. It had been some time since there were new residents at Sage Gardens and she was a little rusty at making her welcome muffins. She wasn't a whiz in the kitchen by any stretch, but it was the one recipe she had learned to master. As she straightened out the basket she smiled to herself. She always enjoyed having new neighbors. It was an opportunity to get to know new people. As a retired journalist her mind always sought out the story.

Once the basket was settled she picked it up and headed out of her villa. The new residents had moved in on the other side of the retirement community so it was a bit of a walk. She didn't mind as the weather was nice. As she walked she thought about all of the positive things she could tell the new residents about Sage Gardens. She loved welcoming new residents as there was so much about Sage Gardens to love. Not only were the residents provided with full house and lawn maintenance, there was a recreation hall, a newly built café, leisure facilities, weekly activities, and a nurse on site in case of any medical needs. In fact if people didn't want to, they didn't even need to leave Sage Gardens. She was lost in thought about the few good friends she'd made during her time at Sage Gardens when someone walked up beside her.

"Morning Samantha."

Jo's cheerful voice elicited an immediate smile from Samantha. "Morning Jo." She paused to take a look at her friend. She was as beautiful as always, and though she only wore jeans and a loose-fitting top she looked fabulous.

"What is that amazing smell?" Jo tried to peek under the towel that covered the basket to keep the heat inside.

"Blueberry muffins." Samantha eased the basket into her other hand to protect it from Jo's investigating fingertips. "We have new neighbors!"

"Oh, I didn't realize that you still did that. How sweet. Who are the new neighbors?"

"Newlyweds. Valda and Roger."

"Newlyweds? At our age? I couldn't even imagine." She shook her head. Samantha bit into her bottom lip.

"I don't think it would be so bad."

"Really?" Jo narrowed her eyes. "I could see dating here and there, but marriage? No, I think I'm way beyond the patience needed for that."

"I don't know. It just seems like it would be easier now. I'm retired, I have a lot of free time. No kids to worry about, no work schedules to work around, not much to stress about when it comes to bills. It would be nice to have someone to just spend time with. Someone warm, and loyal."

"You know what else is warm and loyal? A dog. And the dog won't lie or run off with someone else."

"Very funny, Jo." Samantha grinned. "Actually, maybe you're right, a dog would be nice."

"See?" Jo laughed. Samantha tilted her head towards the villa in front of them. "This is it."

"Well, those muffins smell so good that now I'm starving. Do you want to go to lunch after you spoil the new residents?"

"I'd love to." Samantha started up the walkway. "You should come with me, it never hurts to meet new people."

"Speak for yourself, I'm more of the introverted type."

Samantha had to agree with that. Jo stuck to just about the same three friends and showed no interest in making more. Samantha was the social butterfly. To her, strangers were just friends she hadn't met yet. Jo tagged along behind her as she walked up to the door. Samantha noticed that there were a few moving boxes folded up on the porch as well as an old pair of sneakers. With a swift knock she prepared her widest smile. It faded a bit when no one answered. There was a car in the driveway so she suspected that someone was there. She knocked again, then smiled again. The door swung open. A man in his sixties stared at her.

"May I help you?"

"Hi, my name is Samantha, and I just wanted to welcome you to the neighborhood."

"Roger, who is it?" A woman stepped up beside him. Her sleek, chocolate brown hair was cut mid-cheek which gave her a youthful look. Narrowed eyes settled on Samantha. "What are you selling?"

"I'm sorry, I'm not selling anything. I know

you're just getting settled in and I don't want to interrupt, but I brought you these. If you have any questions about the community or the area I'd be happy to answer them."

"Oh, how nice of you." Valda reached out and took the basket from Samantha. "I am carb-free, but I'm sure my husband will just gobble these down."

"Do you have an allergy?" Samantha's eyes widened. "That must be so tough."

"No, I'm just always trying to keep a trim figure." She swept her eyes up and down along Samantha's frame which had become a bit more voluptuous over the years. Samantha nodded and did not allow her smile to falter.

"You look fantastic."

"Thanks. You're so kind. Isn't she kind, Roger?" She looked over at her husband with a lazy smile.

"So kind. But, we're in the middle of unpacking and all of that, sorry we can't offer you anything to drink." His steel gray eyes stared straight into Samantha's. "We value our privacy."

"Roger!" Valda rolled her eyes and touched the necklace that hung around her neck. Jo was still behind Samantha and did her best not to be noticed by the couple, however a flash of light caught her eye. She looked up to see that the source of the flash was the necklace that hung from Valda's neck. The gold chain lacked sheen and the setting that held a large diamond was quite dated. Jo stared for a long moment.

"Jo? We're going." Samantha drew her attention. Jo looked back at the necklace just in time to see the door on its way to being closed. She shook her head.

"Not the friendly sort I see."

"Not at all." Samantha shrugged. "But my good deed is done for the day, and now we can go get some good eats."

"Perfect."

Samantha walked ahead of Jo with quick,

peppy steps. Jo lingered for a moment as the memory of that necklace stayed in her mind. When she turned to walk away from the door she heard loud voices inside the villa. Samantha was already part of the way down the sidewalk and hadn't noticed that Jo hadn't kept up with her. Jo leaned closer to the door to hear what the argument might be about.

"I've told you a thousand times not to wear that necklace."

"You said not to wear it outside, I wasn't outside."

"You came to the door!"

"So what?" Valda shouted. "Why did you even give it to me if I'm not allowed to wear it? Roger, you're so crazy sometimes."

"I'm crazy? I'm crazy? Do you know what someone would do to you to get that necklace off your neck? You need to use your head once in a while, Valda!"

"Jo!" Samantha waved to her. "Let's go or

we'll miss the specials!"

Jo listened a moment longer, but all she heard was the slam of a door. That seemed to end the argument. She turned and walked down the driveway to Samantha. As she did she reasoned the argument away in her mind. It just seemed like any other married couple to her. As she fell into step beside Samantha she frowned.

"Do you think that they're going to stay long?"

"I hope so. It's always best to have the same neighbors around."

"Maybe." Jo glanced back over her shoulder. The pair settled into Samantha's car for the short drive to the nearby diner. Jo gazed out the window as her mind filled with memories of the past. Samantha chattered on about a play that was opening the next weekend. Jo didn't hear a word of it. When Samantha parked and looked over at her Jo realized that her friend had asked her a question.

"What did you say?"

"Do you want to come with me to the play this weekend? I was thinking of inviting Eddy and Walt, too."

Jo cracked a smile at that. "I could see Walt enjoying it if he is equipped with antibacterial everything, but Eddy will end up snoring."

"Well, maybe some of the culture will seep into his subconscious." Samantha laughed.

***

The diner wasn't crowded as they were late for breakfast and early for lunch. A familiar waitress waved to them and pointed out a table for them to sit down at. Once they were settled Samantha handed Jo a menu. Jo was too lost in thought to notice. She blinked when Samantha tapped the top of her hand with the menu.

"Oh thanks."

"Where are you in your head?" Samantha smiled. "Out in your garden I suspect."

"No, not the garden today." Jo smiled and opened her menu. She did spend a lot of time with her hands in the dirt, but at the moment her mind was focused on the necklace. With a history of being a cat burglar she was quite familiar with valuable jewelry. However, she still couldn't place exactly where she had seen that necklace before. It did however ignite an eagerness in her that made it seem very important. They placed their order then waited for the food.

"Can you believe that there is going to be a movie based on the life of the founder of Sage Gardens? I had no idea the man was so intriguing," Samantha said trying to work out if Jo was listening.

"Hm." Jo nodded. She tapped one foot under the table and swept her gaze around the diner. It was starting to get a little more crowded as it neared the lunch rush.

"Jo, are you listening?" Samantha frowned. "Something really has you distracted."

"I'm sorry, Samantha, I'm just going to the restroom real quick before the food gets here."

"Okay." Samantha took a sip of her water.

While Jo was in the restroom Samantha looked around the diner. She loved to people-watch. To her each person had their own interesting story that was just waiting to be investigated. Her gaze settled on a man perched on a bar stool. He had his back to her. His shoulders were broad, but his chest tapered down to a very slender waist. She admired the shape of his back for a moment until the bar stool swiveled. She tried to look away before he could catch her looking at him, however it was too late.

He gazed at her from behind sunglasses. She noticed a jagged scar from the slope of the corner of his mouth to the base of his hairline. She forgot she was staring as she pondered what could cause a scar like that. He cleared his throat and she jumped in her chair. When she grabbed her glass of water she nearly knocked it over. By the time she set it right on the table the man on the bar stool was gone. He left her with an odd feeling of unease in the pit of her stomach. She looked around the restaurant for any sign of him. Jo sat back down at the table.

"Is something wrong, Samantha?"

"No. I just had this strange feeling about someone," she said. "Just one of those odd moments."

"I have plenty of those." Jo nodded. As they enjoyed their meal both women were distracted. By the time they finished and the waitress retrieved the plates their halfhearted conversation came to a full halt.

"I think it's nice of you to make those muffins for people, Samantha. Sometimes I wish I was a little more social like you. But I guess I am just used to being by myself." Jo stood up from the table.

"Well, you're not by yourself anymore." Samantha linked her arm through Jo's and smiled at her.

Jo was a little surprised by the warmth she felt within her. She smiled back at Samantha. The two spent a little time in town window-shopping and then headed back to Sage Gardens to share a light dinner at Samantha's.

"Want to take a walk?" Samantha cleared the plates.

"I'd love to. I've heard there's going to be a full moon tonight."

"It's late enough, we might get a glimpse of it." Samantha left the dishes in the sink and the two walked out the door.

"One of the things I love the most about Sage Gardens is how easy it is to take a walk here. Plenty of sidewalks, a good amount of lighting, and just a general feeling of safety."

"I do like that, too," Jo agreed and swept her gaze along the sidewalk. Even though Sage Gardens was a quiet retirement community she was always careful about where she was and who might be near.

"Do you have the energy for the full loop?" Samantha glanced over at Jo. "It's so beautiful out."

"Absolutely. After that delicious meal we just had I need to walk it off."

"Oh please, you don't have an ounce of extra weight on you."

"You'd be surprised. Retirement is certainly making me go soft. I used to train in the gym all the time." She left out the fact that it was a gym in prison. "I haven't even been to do Judo in almost six months."

Samantha laughed and shook her head. "I can't imagine doing Judo even six years ago. You're much more limber than me, Jo."

"Trust me, it was just an outlet for my aggression." Jo grinned. "Society frowns on flipping men over your shoulder for fun unless it's in a class environment."

"Now, that might be fun!" Samantha laughed so loud that she covered her mouth to keep from disturbing the early-to-bed residents. It wasn't her laughter that woke them however, it was a piercing scream that filled the otherwise quiet evening. It startled Samantha so much that she grabbed Jo's arm and tugged her towards her in a protective embrace. She was sure that the scream came from inside the villa of the new neighbors.

"What was that?" Jo glared at the villa. "Do you think someone is hurt?"

"I think something terrible has happened." Samantha released Jo's arm and headed straight for the front door of the villa.

"Samantha wait! You don't know what might be happening inside!" Jo jogged to catch up with her. "Remember, Roger said they value their privacy. What's going on is their business."

"Not with a scream like that." Samantha started to knock on the door, however the moment that her knuckles touched the wood the door swung open. In the front hallway not far from the door, Roger's body filled the passage. As Samantha watched he dropped to his knees. Only then did she see the shiny, black high heel jutted out in an odd direction across the floor. She rushed forward and looked over Roger's shoulder to find Valda sprawled out on the floor face up. Muffin crumbs covered her mouth, and she clutched the remainder of the muffin in her right hand. She stared vacantly at the ceiling. It was clear she was dead.

Chapter Two

Samantha's eyes moistened with tears. She turned right into Jo's arms who waited to console her. Jo was shocked herself as she had experienced many things, but the sight of death was not common for her. She looked over at Roger who had stood up from his wife's side and now paced back and forth, his eyes wide.

"Did you call for an ambulance?" Samantha gasped.

"Of course I did! What good will it do?" He glared down at her. "She's dead!"

Samantha sniffled and pulled away from Jo. "How did this happen?"

"She must have choked. She's got so much of that darn muffin crammed in her mouth." Roger crouched down beside her again. "Oh Valda, oh Valda." He took her hand in his and brushed away some muffin crumbs. "I should have been here, maybe if I had been here I would have been able to help her." He continued to mutter his regrets as the police arrived.

"Step aside, please." One of the officers brushed Samantha and Jo away from the woman's body. Roger was immediately pulled aside by another officer. Medics followed the officers, however they only established that Valda was dead. The lead officer assessed the scene, then he joined another officer and Roger in a corner of the living room.

"We need to get out of here, Samantha." Jo tugged at her arm and looked around at all of the police officers. There were only a few, but to her it seemed like thousands. "Let's go. There's nothing we can do here."

"What if the police want to question us?" Samantha continued to stare at Valda's body, more specifically the crumbs that covered her mouth.

"That's what I'm afraid of, Samantha. You know how I am with cops." Jo shifted with an antsy energy from one foot to the other.

"All right, all right." Samantha started to turn towards the door. Before she could reach it one of the officers blocked her way.

"Miss?" The lead officer called out to her. Jo slipped out the door without the slightest hesitation. Samantha found it impossible to walk away from the officer's command. "Are you the one who supplied the muffins?"

"Yes." Samantha swallowed hard. She couldn't imagine that her attempt at welcoming new neighbors had led to an untimely death.

"And why are you here now?" The officer whipped out his notepad.

"I was walking past the villa and I heard Roger scream. I wanted to make sure that everything was okay."

"You're a friend of the deceased?" The officer scribbled on his notepad.

"No, not really. They just moved in. I brought the muffins to welcome them." The officer looked up at her with slightly parted lips.

"Okay," he said slowly and then made another note on his notepad.

"Am I free to go?"

"Sure. Unless you poisoned the muffins." He smiled. Samantha stared at him. His smile faltered. "You didn't, did you?"

"No, I didn't." Samantha glared at him.

"Then you're free to go. I'll be in contact if we need any more information from you." As Samantha stepped out the door she overheard Roger's heated words to another officer.

"It's quite obvious she choked. No one else was in the house."

Samantha found Jo loitering at the end of the driveway as far from the police cars as she could get.

"What took you so long?" Jo looked at the villa nervously.

"The officer was quite interested in my

muffins." Samantha wrung her hands. "I'm afraid they're going to think I was involved. Roger was shouting at one of the officers when I left. They must have been asking him some upsetting questions."

All of a sudden Jo remembered the necklace. "Samantha, I have to go back in there."

"Huh? You couldn't wait to leave." Samantha looked at her strangely.

"I have to look for something that should be in there. I need to see if it is or not."

"Okay." Samantha followed her up the walkway to the villa. An officer blocked the door from any nosy residents.

"I need to get in for just a second." Jo cleared her throat.

"No, you don't." The officer crossed his arms. He was wide enough to block the entire door.

"I left something inside, please, the key to my villa. I have to get it." Jo tried to look calm. Her heart pounded. To speak directly to a police officer was enough to make her break out in a sweat. It had taken her quite some time to get comfortable with Eddy, even though he was already retired from the force when she met him. The officer looked over his shoulder at the lead officer and then nodded.

"All right, but make it quick. The scene needs to be contained in case there is any evidence of a homicide."

Jo thought that was a little strange. Why would they suspect homicide when it was so clearly an accidental death? She didn't want to ask any more questions than she needed to, however. She crouched down near the body under the pretense that she was searching for her key. What she was actually looking for was the necklace that Valda had worn that morning. As she suspected the necklace was gone. There was a red mark on the curve of her neck, but Jo imagined that could have been caused by the woman clawing at her neck if she had truly choked.

"Excuse me, why are you in here?" Roger

paused behind Jo. Jo looked up at him.

"Did you find anything missing? Do you think it was a robbery?" She searched his eyes.

"No, there's nothing missing, other than my wife." Roger's eyes moistened. "Why would you even ask that? I don't understand why everyone is acting like this isn't the simple tragic death that it is."

"I'm sorry, I was just asking." Jo stood up. "I didn't mean to upset you. But are you sure that nothing is missing?"

"I appreciate your concern, but no nothing is missing." He frowned. "Do I know you?"

"I was here this morning." Jo cringed and resisted reminding him about the muffin delivery. "I noticed that your wife was wearing..."

"Ma'am, you need to leave the scene now," the officer at the door commanded her. "Did you find your key?"

"Oh yes." Jo looked over at him and nodded. When she looked back at Roger the lead officer had pulled him over to the corner again. Jo thought about the argument she had overheard that morning. She stepped out of the villa and joined Samantha.

"There's something very strange going on here."

"Stranger than a woman dying on the very same day she moved in here?" Samantha shook her head. "That is terrible luck."

"Strange as in, this might not be accidental."

"What makes you think that?" Samantha looked at her with surprise.

"I'm not sure just yet. I'll let you know if I figure anything out. Are you going to be okay to get home?"

"Sure." Samantha nodded.

"Okay. I'll see you tomorrow."

"Don't forget that we are meeting Walt and Eddy for breakfast at the café."

"Uh huh." Jo nodded but she barely heard her

words. Her mind was on the missing necklace.

Chapter Three

At breakfast the next morning the café buzzed with conversation about Valda's unexpected death. Jo listened closely to the comments around her, but she heard no mention of the necklace that she believed was missing. Perhaps she and Samantha had been the only ones to even see it, if Samantha had even noticed it. The general gist of the conversation was sympathy for Roger and the tragedy of an accidental death. People did whisper about the muffins being made by Samantha, however. Jo noticed that the café grew quiet when Samantha walked in the door. She rushed over to the table to join Jo.

"They all think I poisoned her." Samantha grimaced. "Why would they think that?"

"They don't think that, Samantha. It's just a juicy tidbit for them to discuss. None of them would ever dare to say it to your face."

"Maybe not, but that doesn't change the fact

that it was indeed my muffin that was in her mouth."

"Sure, but it could have just as easily been a piece of apple. She could have choked on anything."

"I know you're just trying to make me feel better, but I don't even want to think about how she died."

"Well, what about her necklace? Do you remember seeing it?" Jo leaned across the table and lowered her voice.

"Necklace?" Samantha shook her head. "I'm not sure. Was she wearing one?"

"She was wearing one when we brought the muffins, but not when she died."

"Huh. Well, maybe she took it off for the evening?"

"Maybe." Jo narrowed her eyes. She recalled the argument Valda had with Roger. Perhaps Roger had insisted that she put the necklace away. Why else would he not mention it to the police?

"It's not just any necklace, it's a very valuable necklace. I'm sure of it." Jo quietened down as she noticed the two men that approached their table. The taller of the two was Walt. His thin frame was immaculately clothed as usual in a sweater and pleated pants. The larger and slightly shorter of the two was Eddy. His balding head was covered with a fedora as usual, and his eyes narrowed slightly at the corners with suspicion. The two men settled themselves at their table.

"Good morning, Samantha, Jo." Walt smiled at both of them.

"Samantha, Jo." Eddy nodded at them and then waved his hand at the waitress for some coffee. "What happened last night?" Eddy looked at Jo. "We just heard that there were some cops here last night. Now you're talking about a necklace? Was there a robbery?"

"Yes." Jo met his eyes.

"No." Samantha raised an eyebrow at Jo. "There was an accidental death. Valda, the new resident."

"Well, accidents do happen," Walt commented.

"Jo and I were there when her husband found her. We heard him scream so we went to check on him." Samantha's eyes filled with tears. Jo handed her a napkin. "It was not your fault, Samantha."

"Why would it be?" Eddy looked over at Samantha and then back at Jo.

"There's a bit of a problem," Jo explained.

"What problem?" Eddy accepted the coffee the waitress brought with a short thank you.

"The woman who died, she and her husband Roger just moved in. So Samantha took them some muffins."

"Sure, she always does." Eddy shrugged. "Why is that a problem?"

"Because Valda died with a muffin in her mouth." Jo cringed.

"Now the police probably think I had something to do with her death!" Samantha wiped at her eyes.

"They think you poisoned the muffins?" Eddy asked.

"Since the preliminary reports haven't come in yet, they can only go on what they saw at the scene. What they saw was a muffin. She might have just died of natural causes, but one of the officers mentioned the muffin being poisoned, but it was probably an off-color joke," Samantha said.

"That's absurd. Maybe she choked?" Eddy suggested.

"That is the presumed cause of death." Jo nodded.

"That is precisely why I only open my mouth a certain amount and chew every bite of food at least twenty times before I swallow," Walt explained. "You may think it's silly, but I haven't choked, have I?"

Eddy looked over at Walt. "So, how many times do you swish your tea?"

"Four. Oh." Walt frowned. "You were teasing me weren't you? It's not funny. You never know when a tea leaf or a portion of the cup might have broken off."

"Why do you think it was a robbery, Jo?" Eddy shook his head. "Are you saying she was eating a muffin, then a robber broke in, and she choked?"

"No, that's not what I'm saying." Jo frowned. "Keep your voice down."

"Oh, I'm sorry I didn't realize this was a secret." Eddy held her gaze across the table. "So, why do you think it was a robbery?" He was not about to allow her to avoid the question.

"Because when we delivered the muffins earlier in the day she had a beautiful necklace on. It had to be an antique. When she died, she was not wearing it."

"And the husband? Did he say the necklace was stolen?" Eddy swept his gaze around the café in search of Roger.

"No. He said nothing was missing." Jo sighed. "But that doesn't make any sense."

"It makes perfect sense." Walt wiped his mouth carefully though he had only taken a sip of his tea. "If she died with an expensive necklace on he probably took it off. If there is even a suspicion of a crime the body and everything she was wearing would be taken as evidence. He might have taken it off to prevent it from getting lost in the system."

"He's right." Eddy nodded. "I've seen people pry rings off dead fingers before the body bag is zipped up."

"Oh, that's so cold." Jo grimaced.

"It's logical." Walt pointed out. "Human life is a great loss, no need to compound it with financial loss."

"I don't think she choked." Samantha's voice interrupted them as she wadded up her napkin. All of the attention at the table focused on her.

"Why not?" Eddy set his coffee cup down on the table. Before Samantha could answer the waitress arrived to take their order. Once their orders were placed Jo jumped in before Eddy could.

"So, why do you think that Valda didn't choke?" Jo frowned. "She clearly had muffin in her mouth. Maybe she got a piece stuck in her throat and couldn't get it out."

"Of course it's possible, but what bugs me is that she specifically told me she was carb-free. Why would a woman who was carb-free eat a muffin?"

Eddy stared at her blankly. "What is carb?"

"Try to keep up, Eddy. I do remember her saying that, Samantha, but she could have been lying. Maybe she was just trying to put you down for bringing the muffins. You know how some people are, they can't be pleased with anything you do."

"Maybe." Samantha nodded. "Although, I

tend to think that there are much easier ways that she could do that. Claiming to be carb-free is very specific."

"Well, try not to worry, it will get worked out." Walt reached out and touched Samantha's shoulder. "I'm sure it was not your muffins. Even though there are many poisons that can easily be hidden in foods."

"Walt, you're not helping." Jo lifted an eyebrow.

"Oops. Sorry." Walt picked up his tea.

"Now, just wait a minute. We have a situation where a woman might not have choked, and her necklace may or may not have been stolen. That's not very much to go on," Eddy said.

"No, it's not, and it doesn't add up does it?" Samantha pursed her lips.

"Maybe we're looking for a crime where there isn't one?" Walt looked between his three friends. "It's not as if we haven't done that before."

"Good point," Samantha agreed. "It's possible

I'm just feeling so guilty about her choking on my muffin that I am trying to create another reason for her death."

Jo was silent. The waitress delivered their food. Jo poked at her eggs. Maybe they were right about Valda's death being accidental, but that didn't mean that the necklace wasn't stolen. The necklace. The necklace. She couldn't get the image out of her head. She knew that it was important for some reason. She just couldn't place why.

***

After they finished breakfast the four friends went their separate ways. Jo tried to calm her mind by pulling out some weeds in her garden. The flash of the sunlight against the flower petals reminded her of the flash of the light against the diamond necklace. When her cell phone rang she dropped her pruning shears. With a sigh she tugged one glove off and answered the phone.

"Jo, it's me Samantha."

"Samantha? Are you okay?" Jo noticed strain

in her voice.

"Listen, I just got a call from the police. I have to go in and give a statement." Her voice trembled as she spoke. "Apparently there is some evidence that foul play may have been involved in Valda's death!"

"I knew it!" Jo sat upright and stared hard out across her garden.

"Knew what? That I poisoned the muffins? I didn't!"

"No, I knew that she was murdered. Someone killed her for that necklace, I'm sure of it."

"Jo, forget about the necklace! Are you even listening to me? I might get arrested for murder."

"It's going to be okay, Samantha. You're not going to get arrested. They probably just want to know what was in the muffins or if you saw anything suspicious. You should take Eddy with you when you speak to them. In the meantime I'll try to drum up some suspects that might have been interested in that necklace. You may not believe me, but I am certain it was stolen."

"If it was stolen then why wouldn't Roger report it?" Samantha sighed.

"Because either he knew that it was stolen, or he stole it himself. It's illegal to be in the possession of stolen goods."

"Wait, are you saying that you think it was stolen before it was stolen?"

"I think so." Jo frowned as she tried to keep up with Samantha's train of thought. "It would explain why he didn't want her wearing it outside. If it was a known stolen item he could get in a lot of trouble if they are caught with it."

"Oh no, Jo."

"What?"

"What if Roger killed her?" Samantha said. "So that he could collect insurance money, plus keep the necklace?"

Jo nodded. "That makes sense except I don't think he would have been able to insure stolen goods. But I heard them arguing about the necklace after you dropped off the muffins."

"You did? Why didn't you tell me?"

"Well, at the time we thought she had just choked to death. I didn't think there was a reason to mention it. It was just your average argument. But now I wonder if that was the final straw for Roger?"

"I'm not sure, but we need to figure out if Valda was murdered and by whom. Otherwise I might be spending a lot of time behind bars."

"Try not to worry, Samantha, you've covered enough crimes to know that it takes a lot to convict someone of murder."

"Actually, I've seen the opposite. I've seen several people who I believe might be innocent locked away on circumstantial evidence. Why do you think I'm so worried?"

"Just do your best to stay calm. Make sure that you take Eddy with you."

"I will." Samantha hung up the phone. Jo held

the phone in her hand for a few moments. If the police were leaning towards murder that meant that the medical examiner had turned up something unusual in relation to the death. It was clear that the woman hadn't been attacked as there was no sign of a struggle. Whoever did kill her did so with enough intelligence to make the scene look like an accident. Roger was the first thought that crossed her mind. He was after all the husband, which made him a strong possible suspect to begin with, but there was one thing that Jo knew about Roger that the police didn't. He was also either a criminal, or at the very least associated with criminals. That was the only way that he could have gotten his hands on the necklace.

Chapter Four

Samantha stared out through the windshield of the car. Ever since Eddy picked her up to take her down to the station he had been in quite a bad mood. In fact, he had repeatedly told her that she was to be extremely cautious about how she spoke to the officers and what she told them. For what felt like the thousandth time he repeated the same statement.

"I wish you had never spoken to the officer at all." Eddy jammed on the brakes as a car pulled out in front of him. The traffic that sunny day was intolerable.

"Why wouldn't I?"

"You shouldn't have admitted to delivering the muffins."

"I should have lied? Wouldn't that make me look more guilty?" Samantha looked over at his reddened cheeks and furrowed brow.

"Look Samantha, as a former officer of the law I would never tell you to outright lie to the police, I mean they are just trying to do the best job that they can. But in this case you outright implicated yourself. How do you even know it was one of your muffins? Her husband or someone else could have switched one when she wasn't looking. You don't know."

"I didn't think it mattered at the time." Samantha sighed and looked down at her hands. She was shocked when Eddy reached out and took one.

"You're right. I'm sorry. You shouldn't blame yourself. But when you go in there and talk to these officers it's important that you say as little as possible. Don't lie, don't evade, but just answer what they ask and nothing more."

"Okay. I will." Samantha swallowed hard. Eddy withdrew his hand quickly as if he had just noticed what he'd done and turned into the parking lot of the police station. In contrast to the packed roads it was not nearly as crowded. They walked into the police station together, but Eddy remained in the waiting area while Samantha was led off to a room for questioning. Eddy would have attempted to follow her, but he had something else in mind. He sat casually in one of the chairs until he spotted the person he was looking for.

"Chris!" Eddy stood up and walked towards the man in a short, white lab coat. Chris turned to look at Eddy with a smug smile.

"I wondered how long it would be until I heard from you."

"You did, why?" Eddy shook his hand.

"I saw the location of the recent DOA. I figured you'd be interested."

"Is there anything you can tell me about it?"

"Come into my office." Chris gestured to a room encased in glass and filled with technical equipment. Eddy nodded and followed after him. Chris closed the door behind him.

"They've got my friend, Samantha, in here to

talk about her muffins."

"Oh no trust me, that's not why she's here." Chris put an x-ray paper up on a light box to the side of his computer. Eddy could see that it was a pair of lungs.

"Then why is she?"

"Because the DOA came in as a choking victim and is now classified as a potential homicide."

"Why?" Eddy's eyes widened. "I thought it was clear that she choked."

"It's clear that she suffocated."

"Can't someone suffocate from choking?"

"It's not exactly the same. You see for someone to die from choking normally whatever they are choking on is either blocking their airway or has been aspirated into their lungs. Valda had muffin crumbs in her throat, nothing she would choke on, and her lungs were clear."

"But Samantha said her mouth was full of muffin."

"Samantha was right. Nearly an entire muffin in fact. But there is good reason to believe that muffin was not there when she died, but was placed there after the fact."

"Wow! Someone killed her and then shoved a muffin in her mouth to cover it up?"

"That's one theory. Another is that she had some other medical event just as she took her first bite. Either way, it's clear that Valda was dead before she tasted the muffin. There was no muffin in her stomach, and none further down in her throat, and as I said, no remnants of anything in her lungs."

"So, this was very likely a murder."

"Yes, I would say that."

"That doesn't explain why Samantha is here."

"Samantha is here because they feel she might know something about the crime. She was at the home of the deceased twice on the same day that the victim died. They're hoping she might have seen or heard something unusual. You know how some officers can be when it comes to questioning, they might shake her up a bit, but in general she is not considered a suspect."

"That's a relief." Eddy sighed. "I'm sure she will be happy to hear that."

"Maybe she'll make us some muffins." Chris winked at Eddy. Eddy stared at him for a moment and then chuckled.

"She probably will. Do they have any suspects?"

"Nothing solid just yet. We'll know more when the full exam is completed."

"You'll let me know?"

"Sure I will, Eddy," Chris replied. "It wouldn't be a normal month if I didn't have you getting me in trouble somehow."

"I appreciate it, Chris."

Chris looked over at him. "I don't mind it at all. If it means that someone pays for a crime, even better."

Eddy clapped his hand against Chris' back and walked back into the waiting area. Just as he reached it Samantha was on her way out as well. She cast a troubled look over her shoulder and then turned to Eddy.

"Get me out of here."

"You've got it." Eddy placed his hand lightly on the small of her back and steered her out of the police station. As soon as she was out, she exploded.

"Really, I will never understand the intimidating tactics that you people use..."

"Hey, wait a minute, you people?" Eddy raised an eyebrow.

"Oh please, you still use them and you know it."

Eddy opened the car door for her. "Would you like to get in? Or is that me being intimidating?"

"Eddy stop! Do you know they questioned me for ten minutes before they even told me that I wasn't a suspect?"

"All right, but they needed to get information from you."

"Like what?"

"Like, did you notice anything suspicious at the scene, did you observe anyone suspicious around the villa, all of that."

"Which I would have answered without them demanding the recipe for my muffins."

"Oh." Eddy grinned. "Chris was hoping you'd make some."

"Ugh, get in the car!" She plonked herself down. Eddy closed the door and leaned in the open window.

"You're using a very intimidating tone to speak to me right now. I feel very intimidated."

"Eddy!"

His laughter wafted through the open window as he rounded the car to the driver's seat. "I'm sorry, I shouldn't tease you."

"It's not funny anyway," she said but she

smiled slightly. "No one should be making me feel like I'm a criminal when I've done nothing wrong."

"So, how do you suggest the police catch criminals? Ask them nicely?"

Samantha huffed and stared out the window. She was relieved not to be a suspect, but not so thrilled at the way she was treated by the investigating officers.

Chapter Five

Jo paced back and forth through the living room. Her mind shifted from thoughts of the murder, to the suspicion around Samantha, and right back to the necklace. She could not shake the memory of it from her mind. The necklace looked so familiar to her as if she might have once owned or worn it, though she knew that was not the case. There were three things that Jo could be certain about. It was old, it was valuable, and it was stolen. She flicked through her phone again.

As a rule Jo had cut contact with most of her friends and connections involved in theft. She thought it was the best way to go cold turkey. However, there were a few people she still had the phone numbers for. She called these people when she had a question about a recent heist, or if she just wanted to chat until three in the morning about the merits of being a thief. Most of the time she didn't call them at all. Now, she felt like she had to. Her hand shook a little as she dialed the number of one of her oldest contacts. Mildred, as she liked to be called though her name was Ronda, was well-known and well-connected in the antique fencing rings. She expected to hear the beep of a voicemail on the phone, instead she heard Mildred's smoke-damaged voice.

"Jo, is that you?"

"Yes it is, Mildred. I'm sorry to call out of the blue."

"That's all you ever do. I think the last time you called me was about two years ago. I was starting to believe that I would never hear from you again."

"I know. Mildred, I wouldn't be calling..."

"If you didn't need something. Don't worry, Jo. I know that you're reformed. So, what can I help you with?"

"I saw this necklace recently. It looked so familiar. I mean the piece itself is beautiful. Definitely antique, and highly valuable."

"Did you steal it?" It sounded as if there was a bit of excitement in Mildred's voice.

"No, of course not." Jo frowned. "But someone did."

"Okay?"

"It's just that I can't figure out where I've seen the necklace before. I feel like I should know, like it's important."

"Tell me more about it."

"The gold chain was old, yellow gold with three, small round diamond studs on either side of the pendant, and the diamond was huge, about three carats. It was princess cut in an antique square mounting."

"Wait, are you talking about the 'Rose Diamond' necklace?"

"It didn't really look like a rose." Jo pictured the setting in her mind. "It didn't have any petals or layers."

"No, it's called the 'Rose Diamond' necklace

because it was owned by a very wealthy family, the Roses, before it was stolen. The patriarch of the family claimed it was a relic from the old world." All of a sudden Jo recalled that there were many thieves after that necklace, but one in particular she remembered very well. Jo had tried to forget about that time of her life, but memories started flooding her mind all at once.

"So, it is stolen!" Jo congratulated herself inwardly. She didn't want Mildred to know how much she actually knew about the diamond.

"If it's the same necklace it is not only stolen but legendary. Don't you remember?" She paused and then cleared her throat. "Oh, I guess you wouldn't. You were in prison at the time of the heist. It was quite the scandal because so many people had been trying to get their hands on the necklace, and then out of nowhere it was snatched."

"Oh, I do remember that!" Jo's eyes widened. "Now, I remember very clearly. I read an article about it in the newspaper. There were several photographs in the newspaper of the necklace. I thought the thief was caught?"

"He was, but the necklace, along with everything else that was stolen that night was never recovered."

Jo rolled her eyes. "Are you trying to tell me that you don't know what happened to the necklace? I don't believe that for a second, Mildred."

"You cannot believe it all you want, but trust me, it was a huge issue. There were several far more experienced thieves that had that target on their list and when the necklace was taken they were very unhappy. They tried to hunt down the necklace, but since it was never found they assumed there must have been an accomplice to the robbery who kept it."

"Any idea who the accomplice was?"

"Nobody ever found out. They must have been a nobody though because otherwise they would have bragged about it or someone would have caught on eventually, you know how thieves can't keep their mouths shut about the big heists."

"True." Jo frowned.

"Anyway, why are you asking about the necklace?"

"I saw it in person, on a woman's neck, the other day."

"You didn't. You must be lying!" The thrill in Mildred's voice was quite clear.

"I'm not. A woman was wearing it, and now that woman is dead, and the necklace is gone."

"What do you mean the necklace is gone?" Mildred asked.

"Stolen I guess."

"Are you saying that the 'Rose Diamond' necklace is in play?" Mildred's voice grew higher and higher with each word she spoke.

"I don't know if it's in play or not, but whoever has it may be responsible for a woman's death. Do you have any idea who that might be?"

"I told you I don't. I know the fence that bought most of the stolen goods from the 'Rose Robbery' though."

"Great. That's a start."

"Sure, when you see Bucky make sure you tell him that I said hi."

"Will do. Thanks Mildred."

"Oh, and Jo, make sure you wear something dingy. He's still the same Bucky."

Jo cringed at the memory.

As Jo hung up with Mildred, Samantha called in.

"Hi Samantha, how did it go?"

"Well, it seems I'm not a suspect anymore, but it was definitely a homicide. Or at the very least a suspicious death."

"Interesting."

"I guess." Samantha sighed. "Eddy just dropped me off at home. I'm all frazzled from the questioning."

"I'm sorry you went through that. Did they mention anything about the necklace?"

"The necklace again? Why are you so fixated on that necklace?"

"It's a very famous necklace. Do you remember an article you wrote about the theft of jewelry from the Rose family?"

"Hm." Samantha paused a moment. "Oh, that necklace! I remember that article. It was featured several weeks in a row because there was such a response. Everyone wanted a chance to try to figure out the mystery. There was no way a necklace like that could just disappear. Not with how much it was worth and what people were willing to do to get it. In fact, as I recall, one of the readers of the newspaper gave the police a solid tip, about a man that could have been the accomplice."

"Oh really? Any chance you remember his name?" Jo asked eagerly.

"Unfortunately, no. But I do know that the

police brought him in for questioning. I'm sure they kept a record of that. However, as far as I know there was never an arrest."

"We need to figure out if this accomplice and Roger are the same man. It's the only way that we're ever going to make any progress."

"I bet Eddy could help with that. He still has some connections that could access the case file. I'll give him a call and ask him to look into it," Samantha suggested.

"Good idea. Samantha, see if you can find a copy of that article somewhere, too. I'd like to read it again."

"I will. But Jo?"

"Hm?"

"I want to ask you something."

"Okay." Jo furrowed her brow. "So ask."

"Is it a murder you're trying to solve, or a theft?"

"Does it matter?" Jo lifted one shoulder in a

shrug. "In the end we'll solve both."

"Even if we find out that Roger is the accomplice, that doesn't prove that he's the one that killed his wife."

"No, it doesn't, but it might get us closer to who did. If someone found out that he was the accomplice and had the necklace in his possession, there are many professional thieves that would be very interested in discovering the location."

"So, we have a wide range of suspects?" Samantha asked.

"I don't think so, not yet at least. Whoever found out about the location of the necklace, if they did, would keep it a secret to prevent other thieves from getting to it first."

"Hm. Interesting."

"Yes, very," Jo agreed.

"I'll call Eddy right now about the name of the man they brought in for questioning."

"Great, see if he can get a picture. I have something I have to do."

"Okay, it's nothing dangerous is it? Do you want me to go with you?" Jo thought about it for a moment. It never hurt to have a second person with her when she visited Bucky in case of an avalanche, but she knew that Samantha was still frazzled from her interview with the police.

"No, it's nothing, I'll be fine. Text me if you get any information from Eddy."

"I will." Samantha hung up the phone. Jo changed into thick jeans, a long-sleeved shirt that she had no particular attachment to, and pulled her long, dark hair up in a ponytail. She experienced a strange desire to dig through her jewelry box. For just a moment she thought that she might have forgotten that she had gotten rid of it. Finally, she fished the silver necklace out from the bottom of the pile.

On the end of the necklace was a delicate charm, a tiny rose. She stared at it for a long moment. She thought about dropping it back into her jewelry box, instead she fastened it around her neck. Then she traded her sandals for heavy duty boots. She tucked her wallet and phone into her pockets and grabbed her keys. She did not want to take her purse where she was going. When she opened the door to step outside she found Walt on her doorstep.

"Hi." He pushed his glasses up along his nose. "Sorry to just show up."

"Walt? I'm about to leave. Is there anything you need?"

"Actually, that's why I'm here. Samantha called me and told me that you might need company."

"Oh no." Jo laughed and shook her head. "Not you."

Walt's eager smile faded. His eyes dropped. "Oh? Someone else then? Eddy is working on some information so..."

"Walt, I didn't mean it like that, I'm sorry. I

just meant that where I'm going is not the kind of place that you would want to be."

"I'm sure I could handle it."

"Walt, trust me, it's not going to be pleasant."

"Maybe it's you that needs to trust me, Jo." He lifted his chin and squared his shoulders. "I am a capable and daring man you know."

Jo couldn't help but smile at his attempt at being stern. "I know you are, Walt. I didn't mean to imply that you're not, but I still don't think it's a good idea."

"Too bad. I'm going, and that's final."

Jo sighed. Now, she didn't find his sternness to be so cute. "If you insist."

"I do." He offered her his arm. Jo shrugged in surrender and took his arm. "I'll drive."

"Oh, no way, I'm driving," Jo said with determination.

"Okay fine. But just this once," Walt said.

Jo laughed and met his eyes. "Are you

turning over a new leaf of stubbornness?"

"I suppose I am. I think it suits me."

"Maybe it does." Jo grinned. "I guess that we'll find out."

Chapter Six

Jo drove with Walt towards Bucky's place. It was quite a long drive, so she flipped on the radio.

"Do you have a favorite station?"

"Not really. I enjoy all music."

"All?" Jo smiled a little.

"All."

Jo tuned into her favorite station and blasted rock and roll music that had more bass than lyrics. Walt slunk back in his seat and looked from the radio to her. To her surprise he began singing along with the music. She laughed as he mimicked an air guitar.

"Walt, I didn't know you had it in you."

"There's a lot you don't know about me, Jo." Walt's hands settled back into his lap. "I hope we can change that."

"Me too." Jo nodded.

They sat in silence for most of the way enjoying the music.

"We're about ten minutes out. Walt, I appreciate you coming with me, but it is probably best if you wait in the car."

"I'm afraid I can't do that. I came with you to ensure your safety, and that is exactly what I will do."

"Do you think I'm not capable of protecting myself? Why, because I'm a woman?" She parked the car and looked over at him. "Isn't that a bit old-fashioned?"

"No, I don't think you're incapable of protecting yourself because you're a woman." He fixed his eyes to hers. "No, I think you are very capable of protecting yourself, but I would like to help so you can relax a little."

Jo narrowed her eyes. "What am I supposed to say to that?"

"Thank you." He opened the door of the car and stepped out. Jo stepped out on the other side and met him in front of the car. "Jo, I won't accept any argument."

"Walt." She met his eyes and offered a half-smile. "Thank you."

"You're welcome." He nodded once and then turned to look at the building before them. It was a simple, small, white building. But all of the windows were blacked out.

Jo paused outside the door and looked over at Walt.

"Are you sure you want to do this with me? Once we get inside it is rather hard to get back out quickly."

"Huh?" Walt frowned. "Does he lock the door?"

"Not exactly."

"Well, whatever it is, I'm here with you, Jo. I can be your protection."

Jo quirked a brow and tried not to smile. She didn't want to hurt Walt's feelings, but she was fairly certain he didn't do well in the role of protector. As she knocked twice on the door and then kicked the base of it once, she hoped that the code hadn't changed over the years. A few minutes later Walt frowned impatiently.

"Maybe no one is here."

Jo glanced at her watch. "Just another minute."

A buzzing sound emitted from inside the door. She nodded and turned the knob. Then she shoved the door as hard as she could. A musty scent spilled out through the door. She squeezed her way through the door. Walt followed behind her. Jo did her best to climb over the piles of papers, magazines, and old records on the floor. She tried not to look at the piles that were crammed to the ceiling all around her. Going to see Bucky was like walking through a crumbling old building, only the bricks were abandoned, useless items. Walt gasped as he struggled to get in behind her.

"What is all of this?"

"This is Bucky's treasure." She spoke in a hushed tone as she knew that Bucky might be able to hear her. "He is a collector."

"Hoarder."

"I don't recommend using that term, he has a very large array of automatic weapons. Of course he probably doesn't know where they are right now, but not a risk I would recommend taking."

"Thanks for the advice."

Walt shuddered as he brushed some garbage on the floor aside with the toe of his shoe.

"Just stay in the middle, don't bump into anything, and don't look down."

"Huh? Why?" Walt looked down at his feet just in time to see a large cockroach race across the floor. It was followed by a flock of smaller bugs. "Oh no, oh dear no, oh my no." Walt pulled a handkerchief out of his pocket and pressed it against his mouth.

"Walt?"

"Just keep going, I'm right behind you." His voice was muffled by the handkerchief. The path narrowed as they walked single file. Jo could tell that Bucky had added quite a bit to his collection since the last time she visited. Every creak and groan of the building made her concerned that she was about to be buried, and very likely become a part of Bucky's collection.

"Who exactly is this man?" Walt cleared his throat.

"He's a fence. The fence really. He's the best person to see if you want to get a good price on stolen goods."

"How can anyone find him?"

Jo grinned. "You have to be somebody, or know someone that is somebody."

"Ah." Walt did his best not to look at the floor as he heard the squeak of a live animal.

They emerged from the narrow hallway of junk into a slightly larger space. In front of them a wall to wall glass counter stretched out. At least it was to be assumed that it was glass. The amount of dust and grime on the surface made it rather difficult to tell for sure. Set back in a giant, leather chair was Bucky. Jo could see that he had likely put on about one hundred pounds. He was a very large man the last time she saw him, but now he was mountainous. He munched happily on crackers as they approached the counter.

"What do you have to offer?" He didn't look up.

"Nothing." Jo paused in front of the counter. "I'm here to get something from you."

Bucky choked on the cracker he crunched. He cleared his throat and peered through his glasses at Jo. "Is that who I think it is? Could it really be?"

"It's me, Bucky."

"Jo. After all these years." He stared at her with disbelief. "I didn't think I would ever see you again. Look at you. Wow, you're still a sight." He stared at her with cracker bits stuck to his bottom lip. "I fell in love with you the first day you climbed over a pile of comics."

"You say that to all the girls, Bucky." Jo crossed her arms.

"Maybe. But I only mean it with a few."

"Mm hm. Great, then you should be able to help me out."

"What do you need from me, Goddess?"

Walt looked between the two of them with a hint of anxiety.

"I need to know about the 'Rose Job'."

"That was Tony's job." He rubbed his hands clean of crumbs and looked at the two over his square glasses. "Where's Tony?"

"I'm not here about, Tony." Jo met his gaze directly. "I'm here to find out about the necklace." He laughed and knocked a few crumbs off his shirt in the process.

"I bet you are. You and about twenty of your friends."

"What do you mean?"

"I mean that this place has been a revolving door of all you so-called professional thieves begging to get your hands on a ghost. Everyone knows that it's a fairytale."

"It's no fairytale." Jo rested her hands on the counter and ignored the droppings of unknown creatures. "I saw the necklace with my own eyes."

"Ha, more lies." Bucky narrowed his eyes. "The Jo I know would not see a necklace like that without stealing it herself."

Walt cleared his throat. "She's not the Jo you knew anymore."

"Please don't help, Walt." Jo shot him a look before she returned her attention to Bucky. "Look, all I want to know is who was working with Tony. Who was his accomplice?"

"How should I know?"

"He sold you all of the stuff."

"And I make it a point to forget the face of

anyone who sells me stolen goods. That's why I've lived so long."

"Which is completely against all scientific and medical explanation." Walt looked around the environment and shuddered at the thought of how many different kinds of mold were probably growing around him.

"You have a problem with my humble abode?" Bucky used his hand to gesture to his surroundings. "Nobody asked you to be here."

"He's just not used to being around so many unique treasures," Jo explained and shot a look of warning at Walt.

"Yes, that's it." Walt lowered his eyes.

"Now Bucky, what about the guy who sold the stuff from the 'Rose Robbery'? Who was he?"

"I didn't care then, and I don't care now."

"Why?"

"The guy who came in here, was a dead man. I knew that from the first moment I looked at him."

"Why?" Jo held her breath.

"Because he had that look. That look of a novice who stumbled onto something much too big for his britches. I can tell you right now that he had no idea how to price the things he had. Tony was the brains, and the brains were locked up. But I was no dummy, I knew he was supposed to have the necklace. I told him that Tony was going to be expecting the money from that necklace. I didn't want him going to any other fence, you know. I wanted to be the one to finally get the 'Rose Diamond'. But he insisted that there was no necklace. He said that when they did the robbery the necklace was nowhere to be found. So, I just gave him what I felt like for what he had, and our business was settled."

"A name, Bucky?" Jo leaned closer despite the putrid scent. "I need to know a name."

"Uh." He rolled his eyes up in his head and smacked his lips a few times. "Dale, no, Dave, no."

He frowned. "I know it started with a D, but my memory, it's just not so great."

"What do you want, Bucky? Do you want cash?"

"You can't give a criminal money," Walt said as he went pale.

"I'm not a criminal, you fool, I'm a businessman. Besides, it's not money I want."

"Then what?" Jo cringed at the possibilities.

"That." Bucky pointed at Jo's chest. Jo blinked.

"What?" Jo said.

"Don't be so crude!" Walt warned.

"The necklace, Jo." Bucky's voice lowered. "You give me that necklace of yours, and I will give you the name."

Jo reached up and clutched the necklace. She recalled putting it on that morning. She hadn't worn it in years. It was a piece of the past that she kept locked away for the sake of compartmentalizing her emotions.

"It's worthless."

"Sure. But I want it."

"Why?"

"You know why. It's a piece of theft history. I can add it to my collection."

"Bucky. That's ridiculous."

"The necklace for a name, Jo. What's it going to be?" He smirked.

Jo reached up and unfastened the necklace.

"Jo, you don't have to do that." Walt moved closer to her. "That's yours."

"Which means that it's mine to give. It means nothing to me, anyway." She held it out to Bucky. Bucky met her eyes.

"I doubt that." He closed his hand around the small charm, but Jo held onto the chain.

"The name, Bucky?"

"All right, fine. The name was Clem. A guy

about your age I guess. Definitely a newcomer. He had no idea what he was doing. I'd be surprised if he has lived this long. But like I said, he didn't have the necklace."

Jo let go of the chain and brushed her hand down the leg of her jeans. "All right. Anything else?"

"Just that he was terrified of going to jail. I told him he should be more scared of Tony, because he wasn't going to be happy taking the wrap for the whole theft alone when Clem was involved. Never saw him again after that."

"Thanks for your time, Bucky." Jo turned away from him.

"If you ever want this back, just let me know, we can work something out." He dangled the necklace for Jo to see.

"Your loss, Bucky, it's worth nothing."

"Maybe, but it's history." He grinned and gazed at it like it was the ultimate treasure. Jo picked her way back through the piles of junk until she made it to the door. Walt followed in her exact footsteps. When she reached the door she had to shove things out of the way that had slid out of place when they had entered. More creatures scuttled into and out of view. Walt reached out a hand to steady himself and placed it right through a spider web.

"Oh no! Out, out the door now!" He nearly shoved Jo through the door. As he did he brushed and swiped at his hand and arm while shaking the rest of his body.

"Walt, are you okay?" Jo stared at him with wide eyes.

"Spider web," he hissed.

"Oh." Jo grinned. "You can't say that I didn't warn you."

"Actually, I can say that. You did not fully inform me of the situation that I was walking into."

"I tried to."

"Hm. Either way I'm glad I was here. Now, do

you want to tell me about that necklace?"

"The 'Rose Diamond'?"

"No. The necklace that was important enough that Bucky wanted it."

"It's not important to anyone but him. Bucky has this weird habit of keeping memorabilia related to thieves. That necklace was a gift to me, so he wanted it."

"From him?"

"No. From someone else."

"Who?" Jo opened the door to her car and settled inside. Walt followed suit. Jo started the car. "Jo, you can trust me you know."

"It's not important." She backed the car out of the parking lot in one swift movement that left Walt breathless with his hands glued to the dashboard. "It's ancient history."

***

After Jo dropped Walt off at his place she continued to her own. Samantha called several times before she answered.

"Did you find out anything?"

"It was nice of you to send me an escort," Jo said.

"Oh, you didn't mind did you? I just thought Walt might enjoy the trip."

"I don't think he did." Jo cracked a smile.

"Well?"

"I found out that the man who brought the items from the 'Rose Robbery' to the fence was named Clem. Does that line up with anything you found?"

"Yes, actually. The man that was brought in for questioning was named Clemson Pick. He was questioned and released without the police finding any evidence of involvement."

"Great." Jo frowned. "I guess that leaves us at a dead end."

"No, it doesn't. I'm texting you a picture now. See what you think."

"Okay. I'll call you in the morning all right?"

"Sure. Are you okay, Jo?"

"I'm fine. Just a little tired."

"Okay. Get some rest."

Jo hung up and waited for the text to come through. When it did, she looked at the picture. She thought it looked very similar to Roger, but it was hard to be sure. Many years had passed. The man in the picture had jet black hair. Roger had very blonde hair. She sent a text back to Samantha agreeing that the picture looked similar to Roger.

"So Roger, were you the thief that robbed so many of the glory of the 'Rose Diamond'?" Jo muttered to herself.

She tapped her phone against her knee and considered her options. Samantha could dig into Clemson's past and figure out a connection, she was sure, but that would take time. Time was something they did not have. Since so many thieves knew about the 'Rose Diamond' necklace, if it became known to them that it had resurfaced,

Roger was in danger if he had it. If he didn't have it, then someone had killed his wife for it.

Jo was sure that she could figure out the truth if she was alone with Roger for any length of time. She decided the best plan of action was to get Roger alone. She needed to find out a little bit more about him. She left her villa with only her phone tucked into her pocket. Casually she walked in the direction of his villa. As she did she noticed a few of her neighbors walking in the same direction. She guessed that everyone was a little curious about what had happened to Valda. Jo noticed Roger step outside. She slowed down so that she would reach his driveway in the same moment that he backed out his car. Just as he hit the road, she stepped close enough to his car to make it seem as if he might have hit her. He hit the brakes and leaned out the window.

"Are you okay? Are you hurt?"

"I'm fine, I'm sorry, I wasn't paying attention." Jo hugged herself as if she was shaken by the near collision.

"No, I didn't see you. I'm sorry." He put the car in park and got out of the car. He walked over to her. "Are you sure you're okay?" He touched her elbow gently.

"I'm fine, I'm just a little shaken up." She sniffed. "I'm sorry, I'm the last person you should be worrying about right now."

"Hey, don't apologize to me. Do you want me to give you a ride home?"

"No, that's the last place I want to be. It's so empty there." She reached up to grasp her necklace only to be reminded that it was no longer there. She rubbed the slope of her neck instead. "Sometimes I just get tired of being alone."

"I can understand that."

"Oh listen to me, lamenting about my problems when you've just lost your wife. I'm so sorry. In fact, would you be interested in having coffee tomorrow? We can meet at the café. If you want to talk, I mean."

"I would love to." Roger's eyes widened.

"Around nine?"

"Perfect. Thanks Roger." She smiled. "You've brightened up my evening."

"See you tomorrow. Jo. Right?"

Jo's heart dropped. She hadn't thought about whether Roger might recognize her. There was a time that she was well-known as a cat burglar. Would he be able to recognize her now?

"Yes. Jo."

"Okay. See you then." He walked back to his car. Jo turned around and walked the other way. She was lost in thought when she nearly walked into Samantha.

"Jo, I know you're up to something." Samantha tried to block her way down the sidewalk. "What were you talking to Roger about?"

"I invited him to coffee tomorrow morning."

"Jo, that's not a good idea."

"I think it is. It won't take much for me to find

out if he's a thief or not."

"He could be very dangerous, Jo. I don't think it's a good idea," Samantha repeated.

"I think that you are being paranoid." Jo smiled sweetly. "I'm having coffee. That's all."

"But there's a good chance that Roger had something to do with the murder, remember? You're going to have coffee with a murderer?"

"I'm going to offer sympathy to a widower." Jo set her jaw. "I will be just fine. Now, if you'll excuse me I need to get home and get some rest."

"Jo, please be careful."

"Samantha, you're always encouraging me to be more social." She winked at her friend as she walked away. She could feel Samantha's gaze following after her. She knew that Samantha was concerned, but she also knew that this was the fastest way to find out the truth about Roger. What Samantha didn't understand, and couldn't, was that as long as that necklace was floating around somewhere thieves willing to kill to get what they wanted, would draw closer and closer. When she settled into bed that night and closed her eyes, the image of the necklace popped into her mind. Maybe, just maybe, a small part of her hoped to be the one that found it once and for all.

Chapter Seven

The next morning Jo woke early. She received a few calls from Samantha, but she ignored them. She didn't want to be talked out of her plan. She dressed quickly and did her best to ignore the fact that her necklace was gone. It brought back some of her best memories, but it also reminded her of a deep pain that she had never been able to shake. When she reached the small café beside the main office she noticed that Roger was waiting for her outside. A smile rose to her lips that didn't feel genuine.

"Be nice Jo, you can do that, just be nice," she muttered to herself before offering her hand to Roger. "Thanks for agreeing to meet."

"My pleasure, but I'm afraid we can't stay here."

"Why not?"

"They're cleaning the floors. The place is shut down for the morning."

"Oh, what a shame." Jo shrugged. "I guess they have to clean some time."

"Still, this has to be the worst time."

Jo wondered if Samantha might have had something to do with the café being closed. She became even more determined to get to know Roger.

"Well, I suppose we could reschedule." She kicked her foot against the sidewalk.

"We could have coffee at my house?" Roger offered a half-smile. "Is that too weird?"

"No." Jo's eyes widened. "No, that's just fine, Roger. Don't worry about anything being weird."

"Great." He brushed his hands against his trousers as if they might be sweaty, then he began to walk across the street to the road that led to his villa. Jo matched his pace. Her heart pounded with a mixture of fear and anticipation. Although she knew it was quite dangerous to go back to his house, especially since no one had any idea that she was, she was thrilled by the thought that she would have a chance to look around for the necklace. Jo suspected that Roger stashed it somewhere inside the villa before he called the police. If that was the case it would likely still be there. As she walked along she kept looking over at him. He looked very much like the suspected accomplice to the robbery, but his hair was blonde. Jo was certain from the picture that the robber she was looking for had dark hair. Did he dye it?

"What do you do for a living, Roger?"

He looked over at her, startled by the question. "Oh, I'm retired."

"Me too." Jo smiled. "I guess I should say, what did you do for a living?"

"I was uh, in antiques. You know, buying and selling."

Jo raised an eyebrow. Was it possible he was a fence? Maybe he wasn't the robber at all, but the man that the robber had sold the missing necklace to. Not that it mattered much to Jo.

"Wow, it must have been fascinating to deal with such valuable and historical objects."

"It was. It was also dusty. Very dusty." He laughed. Jo laughed, too. It seemed like the right thing to do.

"Do you think there is anyone out there that ever knows what treasure they have before they try to sell it in a yard sale?"

"You'd be surprised. Most of the time the moment an elderly relative keels over, the ones who inherited their junk carry it all into a shop to be appraised. Ninety-nine percent of the time it belongs in the dump."

"That's sad, isn't it? To think that all of the items we collect over the years might one day end up in the dump?" She bit into her bottom lip as she realized how insensitive she was being. "I'm sorry if that comment upset you."

"Why would it?" He shrugged. "It's true."

"Well, with Valda passing."

"Oh trust me, none of Valda's things are going

to end up in the dump. The woman had a voracious appetite for all things expensive and fashionable. In fact if you want to take a look through her closet you're welcome to."

"Oh no, I couldn't do that."

"She wouldn't have minded." He grinned. Jo swallowed back a few choice words. His casual nature about his wife's death was another reason to believe that he was involved in her murder. How could anyone offer their wife's clothes within a day of her sudden death?

"Well, that's quite kind of you."

"Jo, you know, you're the first person that reached out to me. It meant a lot to me, considering that we don't know each other at all."

"I just don't want to see anyone go through loss alone."

"I really appreciate that." He paused a moment to look into her eyes. "Maybe moving here wasn't such a bad idea."

Jo did her best to fake a look of affection. She

wasn't sure if it worked out well because he quirked an eyebrow and then walked up the path to the front door. Jo followed after him. Just before she was about to go inside she sent a quick text to Samantha to let her know where she was.

Then she followed him inside. There was no way she could turn down the opportunity to have a look around his house. She might be able to find something that implicated him in his wife's death, even if she couldn't find the necklace itself. As she stepped through the front hallway where Valda's body was found she felt a twinge of guilt. Would Valda approve of her trampling on the carpet where she took her very last breath?

"Coffee? Tea?" Roger smiled.

"Coffee please."

Roger went to the kitchen and set about preparing the coffee. As Jo waited she scanned the living room for any signs of a scuffle. She didn't see anything out of place. She also noticed that there were many tiny touches of what she presumed was Valda's personality throughout the room. What might have been bland was splashed with color. Whatever surface was available was waxed and shiny. In the short time that Valda lived in the villa she had left her mark.

"Here we are." Roger returned with two cups of coffee. The two sat down on the couch. Jo's cell phone rang. She saw that it was Samantha and turned the volume of the ringer off.

"A friend?" Roger leaned a little closer to her.

"Yes. Sorry for the interruption. Roger, you look so familiar to me. It's strange," Jo said, she wanted to see if she could get any information from him.

"That's funny, because you look familiar to me too, Jo. As if I've seen you somewhere before."

"Oh?" Jo glanced away from him. "Perhaps we have crossed paths before."

"Maybe. But I think if I met you before, I'd remember. You're quite beautiful."

Jo's stomach churned. His wife's body wasn't

even in the ground yet. It was easy for Jo to assume that because of his history with antiques and obvious callous nature he likely was the accomplice in the robbery. But was he a killer?

"Excuse me, Roger, do you mind if I use your bathroom?"

"Of sure. It's right around the corner. I'll just clean up our cups."

"Thanks." Jo stood up and made her way around the corner. When she got to the bathroom door she paused and tried to peek into the bedroom. The door was only open far enough for her to see a black box sitting on the edge of the bed. She heard the clatter of cups in the sink and ducked into the bathroom. Once the door was closed she grabbed onto the vanity unit to steady herself. She was disgusted by Roger's behavior. She looked at herself in the mirror and noticed that the medicine cabinet was slightly open. She wanted to look to see if there was any indication that Roger had killed Valda. She titled her head to the side so she could get a closer look. She looked on the top shelf and all she found were toothpaste, bandages, and an assortment of other toiletries, nothing unusual. Then she looked down to the bottom shelf and she spotted a box of blonde hair dye right away. That was it, her heart rate quickened slightly. She didn't think it was Valda's, as her hair was dark. She presumed the dye belonged to Roger, which meant that he might have the dark hair that the suspected thief did.

As good as it was to discover this information it also left Jo a little more nervous. If Roger was the thief, and also a murderer, then she was alone with a very dangerous man. When she stepped back out into the living room, she didn't see Roger. She paused in the center of the room and listened. There was no sound of running water, no sound of footsteps, not even the swish of pant legs. Her heart pounded as she wondered where he might have gone. Just when she was about to leave the villa he stepped out of the bedroom.

"Sorry, I had to take care of something." He smiled. "Thanks for spending some time with me this morning, Jo."

"I enjoyed it." She watched him as he stepped closer to her. "I'm very sorry about Valda. I'm sure that she was a wonderful woman."

"She was all right." Roger shrugged. "As long as she had new clothes and fine wine she was just fine."

"Nothing wrong with enjoying the finer things."

"Do you, Jo?"

"Do I what?"

"Appreciate the finer things?"

Jo tilted her head to the side and studied him. "Why?"

"I just think a woman as beautiful as you, should have something special to wear."

"I'm not sure I understand."

He held out a small red jewelry box. Her heart fluttered. Was it really going to be this easy? Was he just going to hand her the necklace?

"Oh really, this is too much, Roger."

"Please. I'm sure Valda would want it to be worn."

She tried to hide the tremble in her hand as she took the jewelry box from him. She opened it up to discover a silver bracelet with jade beads. It was beautiful, but not what she expected.

"Thank you, Roger."

"I hope that you like it. There's so many things to give away, and I just knew this was meant for you."

"It's very pretty."

"Would you like me to help you put it on?"

Jo met his eyes. She got the feeling that if she declined she might regret it. "Sure." She held out her wrist to him. He ran his thumb along the back of her hand as he positioned the bracelet. Her stomach twisted. She tried to keep a smile on her face so as not to tip him off to the fact that she was absolutely disgusted by his behavior. He fiddled with the clasp for some time before letting go of her hand.

"Now every time you look at it, you can think of me."

"Great." Jo forced her smile to grow wider.

"Maybe we could have dinner sometime?"

"Maybe, Clem."

"Who?"

"Huh?"

"You just called me Clem. My name is Roger."

"Oh right, sorry." Jo frowned. She couldn't believe she had made such a stupid mistake, but she noticed that he didn't even flinch when she called him Clem. "See you soon, Roger." She walked over to the door to let herself out. Roger's friendly expression transformed into something much darker. He didn't speak as she stepped out of the villa and closed the door behind her. The second she stepped out of the villa, Samantha popped out from behind one of the large bushes at the end of the driveway. Jo was so startled she let out a yelp.

"Jo!" Samantha hit her on the shoulder.

"Ouch. Why did you do that?" Jo frowned and rubbed her shoulder. The swat didn't really hurt, but the surprise of the strike was enough to make her heart race.

"How could you go to his house for coffee? That was stupid and dangerous."

"And exactly what you would have done." Jo frowned. "Besides, I found something interesting."

"What?"

"He has blonde hair dye in his bathroom. I also spotted a box on his bed. I think it might have the necklace in it."

"Did you actually see the necklace?" Samantha met her eyes.

"No, I didn't see it. But I'm going to keep looking."

"Well, I have some information to share with

you. That's why I called you first thing this morning, and then again, and then again."

"I'm sorry, I thought you were calling to talk me out of it. I just didn't want to be distracted." Jo glanced back over her shoulder at Roger's villa. "I really thought I would be able to figure out if it was him. I mean with the blonde dye I'm pretty certain, but he barely reacted when I called him Clem by mistake."

"I do really think it's him," Samantha said.

"You know that for sure?"

"No, but I'm almost sure, he just looks so much like the picture. Eddy was able to connect with some friends in the department that got him the transcripts of the questioning. It was clear that they dropped the ball. He had no real alibi and his fingerprints were at the scene of the crime."

"But they let him go? Why?"

"Eddy's not sure. He did mention that bribery was rampant in that particular department. Maybe Clem offered them something that they wanted."

Jo glanced down at the bracelet on her wrist. "I think he's used to bribing people to do what he wants. He gave this to me, it belonged to Valda." She shuddered, she wanted to pull the bracelet off her wrist, but she didn't want to risk Roger seeing her without it, yet. "To think he killed his wife and now he's giving away her jewelry to other women."

"He didn't kill her. At least not according to Eddy and Walt."

"What do you mean?"

"While Eddy was looking into Clem, I mentioned that we thought maybe he had killed Valda. He told me that both he and Walt saw Roger at the buffet."

"Walt, went to a buffet?"

"I know right?" Samantha grinned. "I thought that was odd, too. But Eddy said he talked Walt into it because the meal was cheap and Walt's trying to experience new things. But when they got there he couldn't get Walt to eat anything besides a bread roll. Anyway, they saw Roger there. He was getting a lot of attention as the new resident. Eddy insisted that Roger could not have gotten home in time to kill Valda."

"So, it looks like he is the accomplice, but he is not the killer?"

"Remember, on the night that we found Valda's body, Roger said that he should have been there. Valda was home alone while he was at the buffet. A woman like that probably wouldn't be caught dead at a buffet. Especially seeing as she claimed to be carb-free."

"Good point." Jo ran her hand along her chin. "So, if Roger was at the buffet and Valda was home alone, it's possible that the necklace was the target the entire time. The murder might have just been an unplanned consequence."

"Which means that someone knew Roger had the necklace."

"Or, someone always knew that he did."

"What do you mean?" Samantha paused in front of her villa.

"Look, I was pretty much always a solo thief." She softened her voice as she knew that Samantha probably didn't want to hear too much about her past and she certainly didn't want anyone else overhearing her. "But I learned that if you did a job together, that was a bond, almost like a sibling bond. So, if Tony and Roger did this job together, but Roger kept the jewel of the crime, then Tony has likely been seething about it all of these years. Maybe he put a hit out on Roger from prison?"

"Or maybe..." Samantha took a sharp breath. "Maybe he's out! Think about it. No one was injured in the 'Rose Burglary', so Tony may have finished his time by now, and even if he didn't he might have gotten paroled early."

"Well, if Tony is out then he is going to be our main suspect."

"I'll find out what I can from my contacts. In the meantime, Jo please, stay put. I'll let you know whatever I find out, I promise."

"All right." Jo tugged at the bracelet on her wrist. "I'll keep this on a little while longer in case we need to keep Roger on our good side. But Samantha you have to find out as fast as you can. If Tony is out, he's not going to be satisfied unless he has the necklace and payback. He may still be hanging around waiting for the right moment to strike Roger."

"Who knew thieves could be so dangerous?"

"Most aren't." Jo lifted her chin. A surge of defensiveness caused her cheeks to grow hot. "For most the goal is to get in and out with minimal damage, human or property. But there are some that are reckless."

Samantha stared at her for a long moment. "I wasn't talking about you, Jo."

"I know. I'm sorry. This whole thing has my head spinning." Samantha reached out and gave Jo's arm a squeeze.

"Try not to let it get to you, Jo. This is not your

life anymore. We all have pasts, okay?"

Jo nodded. She swallowed back the words that would point out how different their pasts were. Samantha had been gracious to her about her past from the first time they met. She was very grateful to her friend for that.

Chapter Eight

Samantha watched Jo walk away and then she walked up to her villa. After speaking to Eddy about the Clem connection she felt that solving this case might become very complicated.

Samantha's phone rang as she stepped inside. She answered it with a tired greeting.

"Eddy, what's up?"

"Did you find Jo?"

"Yes, I did. She was in Roger's house."

"Clem's house. Is she crazy? What was she doing in there?" Eddy's voice fluctuated with frustration.

"Jo can handle herself quite well you know, Eddy. But I did talk to her. I told her what you found out, and she asked me to look into Clem's partner, Tony, to see if he is still in prison."

"We're getting into a dangerous position here. Walt told me about the man Jo met with. Bucky is a powerful and well-known criminal. If he thinks we're crossing him we could face some serious consequences."

"I think we need to let Jo take the lead on this one. She has the experience."

"Experience? Of being a criminal? I'm not sure that's the best idea."

"I don't think you have a choice here, Eddy." Samantha flopped down on the couch and closed her eyes.

"Excuse me?"

"You're not in charge here. Yes, Jo has a criminal past. You have a past of being a grumpy and aggressive officer of the law..."

"No one could ever prove that."

"I have a past of getting myself into reckless positions and trying to save murderers from well-deserved prison sentences. Walt, I imagine, has some kind of questionable past, too. The point is, we all draw on those pasts in order to contribute our skills. So, Jo is contributing her knowledge.

She feels that if Tony is out, which I think is possible, he may be on the hunt for Roger."

"If Tony got his hands on that necklace, he's long gone."

"You're probably right. But I'm going to look into it."

"All right." Eddy hung up before she could say another word. She rolled her eyes and nestled down on the couch. No matter how sleepy she was, she had a few phone calls to make. As she dialed the number to one of her contacts she felt a familiar thrill.

It was always fun to investigate.

"Hi Samantha, it's been a while since I've heard from you."

"Hi Tasha, I was wondering if you could get me some information on a prisoner."

"I'm fine thanks, and you?"

"I'm sorry. I was in a rush. How are you, Tasha?"

"Everything is good. What's the name?"

"Tony Farie. Can you tell me if he's been paroled or released?"

"It's going to take me some time to find out since it's near the close of business. Can I call you tomorrow with the information?"

"The sooner the better. I appreciate your help."

"I'll see what I can do."

Samantha hung up the phone and yawned again. She found she got more tired out lately. She made a mental note to schedule a check-up.

A few hours later Samantha woke to knocking on her front door. She blinked away sleep and sat up. Her back was stiff from napping on the couch. Her curtains were still up on the windows, it was dark outside. The knocking came again. She pushed herself to her feet and walked towards the door. When she reached it, she paused. Who would be knocking so late?

"Who's there?"

"It's me, Jo."

Samantha opened the door for her friend. She found Jo dressed in skintight black clothes.

"What are you up to in that outfit?" Samantha swept her gaze up and down then looked at Jo's face.

"I'm going to Roger's place tonight to check it out."

"You mean break in?" Samantha titled her head to the side. "Do you think it's a good idea?"

"It's not like I haven't broken in anywhere before."

"I know that, but this time it's different."

"How?"

"How easy do you think it is to break into a thief's house?"

The question triggered a slew of concerns in Jo's mind. Samantha had a good point. If Roger was who she thought he was he had pulled off an amazing heist.

"I'm prepared."

"What are you looking for exactly?" Samantha asked.

"I want to be sure that the necklace isn't in there. I also want to get a look at his computer. So what if he wasn't there when Valda died? That doesn't mean that he didn't hire someone to be."

"I see you've been working some theories."

"Yes, and the only way to find out what is true or not is to break in and have a look around. You asked me to keep you in the loop, so I am. Did you find out anything about Tony?"

"No, not yet, it's going to take some time."

"All right, well I'll let you know what I find out."

"Oh, no you don't. You're not going anywhere without me."

For once Jo didn't argue. "I could use a lookout."

"Great, I'm perfect for the job. Just let me text

Walt and Eddy to let them know what we're doing."

"No." Jo met her eyes. "Just us. It's an in and out job. It won't be a problem I promise. I really don't have the patience to go through the whole, 'Jo this is too dangerous speech' from either of them. Samantha, we're independent women who have been in plenty of dangerous situations, right?"

"Uh, yeah." Samantha slid her phone back into her pocket. "Yes, you're right."

Samantha and Jo walked to Roger's villa. As they approached the villa all of the windows appeared to be dark. They started to move closer to the villa. Samantha grabbed Jo's arm to stop her.

"There's someone back there, behind the villa." Samantha looked over at Jo with wide eyes. "I saw a shadow."

"Stay here." Jo started to walk around the corner of the house.

"No, Jo don't." Samantha grabbed the crook of her elbow again. "I have a bad feeling about this, please." Jo met her eyes through the darkness. It was clear that her friend was concerned, but Jo was determined to not only find the murderer, but to find the necklace that was stolen. She shook off Samantha's grasp.

"Trust me, I'll be fine. Just stay here." Jo broke away and walked around the back of the house. She moved with stealth and grace. It was easy for her to be silent as she had spent so much time working as a cat burglar, and then isolating herself in prison. When she neared the other side of the house, she saw the shadow. Actually, it was a person, but the person was covered from head to toe in dusty-black clothes, which made the person look like a shadow. Jo was startled by the sight. One of the thieves she had worked with in her early years explained to her that solid-black clothing stood out more than smokey-black clothes. Therefore to blend in, she always wore the same slightly smokey-black clothes. This person wore a similar outfit, which to her meant that the person hidden beneath the mask was an experienced thief. She braced herself for what was about to play out.

"Stop right there!" Jo demanded. The figure froze with fingertips pressed against the glass of the window. "What is your business here?" The figure turned slowly to face her. Jo's heart raced as despite the fact that the person was concealed by a mask, there was something very familiar about him.

"Walk away, Jo, before you can't turn back."

Jo's breath caught in her throat. Her fingers trembled just at the fingertips. "Drew?"

"Don't say my name, you know better than that."

"You did this? You killed a woman?" Jo was so shocked that she forgot to keep her voice low. Samantha rounded the corner just as Drew wrapped his gloved hand around Jo's mouth and pulled her body back against his.

"Jo!" Samantha shouted.

Jo didn't hear her because she was far too occupied flipping Drew right over her shoulder. She slammed his lean frame down hard on the ground, then placed a foot on his chest to keep him still.

"Doesn't look like I'm the one who is going to have a problem with turning back."

"Jo, let me up." He grabbed her ankle and held it tight, but he did not attempt to pull her down. "You have no idea what you're doing here."

"I know exactly what I'm doing," Jo said. She did not look away from Drew. He reached up and pulled his mask up enough to reveal his face. Jo tried not to be moved by it. He had the same baby blue eyes and full lips, the same rigid jawline and thick eyebrows. He looked just as he did when she first met him, aside from a few gray hairs and wrinkles. The memory of their brief, but passionate affair rushed through her mind.

"I'm going to call the police," Samantha said.

Jo's heart rate quickened. She did not want the police to come. She wanted nothing to do with the police, but she didn't want a murderer getting away. She started formulating a plan so she could restrain Drew and escape herself before the police got there.

"You're going to send me to prison? After all of these years? Have you no respect?" Drew asked when she didn't protest at Samantha calling the police.

"I have respect for those that deserve it. Murdering someone gets no respect from me."

Samantha dialed the police while she kept her gaze locked on the two. It was easy to gather their history from their body language and the tension in their voices. What was harder to figure out was whether Jo was angry at him for the murder, or something much more personal.

"I didn't murder anyone!" Drew yanked hard on Jo's leg and knocked her off balance. She flipped to the side and landed on her feet, but

Drew was able to get to his before she could stop him. "You know better than that." He glared at her. "I came here for the necklace, that's all."

"I don't believe you." Jo shifted in a slow circle around him to keep him from running. She could hear sirens in the distance.

"Yes, you do." He smirked a little and took a step towards her. "You believe me, because you know that I would never kill anyone. You know me better than anyone, Jo, years and lifestyle changes don't erase that."

Jo was breathless as he took another step towards her. His demeanor was mild, if not a little seductive. She recalled the amount of times they had celebrated together and the plans they made together for big heists. They never actually did one together, but they dreamed up quite a few adventures.

"I don't know you at all, not anymore."

"Then here." He held out his hands to her. "Tie me up. Do what you will. If you really believe that I killed someone, go ahead and show me." His eyes met hers with a spark of heat. She couldn't look away. "Go on, Jo, show me just what you think of me."

"Jo?" Samantha spoke up and broke the tension between the two. "Do you want me to do it? I have some zip ties in my purse."

"You have zip ties in your purse?" Jo looked over at her with some shock. In that instant Drew took advantage of her distraction and shoved her hard right into Samantha. He bolted into the darkness as Samantha and Jo stumbled over each other in an attempt to untangle.

"He's getting away!" Samantha tried to run after him, but Jo grabbed her hand to stop her.

"Don't bother, Samantha. He's already gone."

With sirens fast approaching, Jo felt her stomach churn. She wanted to run, just like Drew did, just like they had in the past. It was already too late as beams of light arched along the outside wall of the villa and over the grass. Within moments Jo had her hands in the air and Samantha stumbled over her attempt at an explanation. "We saw someone back here, it looked like he was going to break in."

"What are you two doing out so late?" One of the officers asked. Samantha recognized them as two of the officers who had attended the scene when Valda died.

Jo lowered her hands when she saw that no one was going to cuff her. "We went for a walk, to look at the stars," Samantha replied.

"And the man you saw?"

"I didn't see much. It was too dark. I ran after him to try to stop him, but he got away." Jo shrugged. She tried to act casual, but under the surface she was panicking, she hated talking to the police.

"So, what you're saying is you didn't get a good look at the man you thought was possibly breaking in to this villa?" The police officer jotted down a note on his pad.

"Yes, that's what I'm saying." Jo narrowed her eyes.

"And you?" The officer looked over at Samantha. "Did you see his face? Anything about him?"

"She didn't see him until he was running off in that direction." Jo pointed towards the road that Drew ran down. Samantha cleared her throat, but she didn't argue the point.

"Is that true?" The officer tapped his notepad with his pen.

"I didn't see anything but a blur," Samantha stated.

"And what exactly were the two of you doing walking around at this time of night?" The police officer who Jo guessed was just barely above twenty-five addressed her as if she was a teenager hanging out after curfew.

"Walking, like we said," Jo said.

"Just walking?"

"It's a beautiful night." Jo looked up at the stars.

"This is the same villa where a woman died. A woman who you are suspected of poisoning with muffins." The officer looked over at Samantha. "Are you sure that there isn't anything else that you want to tell me? Do you have a reason for returning to the scene of the crime?"

"Excuse me, but it was proven my muffins had nothing to do with her death." Samantha frowned. "It's a small community, it's impossible to go for a walk and not be near someone's villa at some point. I didn't even realize which one it was, since it's so dark."

"So, you were out walking, in the dark, for no particular reason, and ended up catching a man trying to break in, but neither of you saw his face or can give any form of description of him?"

Jo looked sideways at Samantha. She expected her to admit that they had both seen and spoken to Drew, but instead she only shook her head. "Are you going to arrest me for walking and reporting a crime?" Samantha asked.

"No ma'am, not at this time. But I would advise very strongly that you keep your walks to the daylight hours. Understand?"

Samantha nodded without another word. The officer turned back to Jo. "As for you, I'd like to recommend that the next time you see a masked man, run the other way and call the police, don't try to chase him down. You could have been hurt, or worse. Really, you should consider how dangerous something is before you make the decision to run straight for it."

"Yes, officer." Jo folded her arms across her chest and settled her gaze on him. "Next time I'll call the police instead of doing their job."

"Jo!" Samantha exclaimed.

"Sorry." Jo lowered her eyes. "I'm sorry, I didn't mean it that way." She held up her hands in mock surrender.

The officer shook his head and walked away.

"Jo, are you trying to get us thrown into jail?" Samantha asked.

"I'm sorry, he got under my skin."

"We have to talk, Jo," Samantha said.

"What's going on here?" Eddy crossed the grass to reach them. "I heard the sirens and came to check it out. It's not Roger is it?"

"No, it's not Roger. Let's go before that officer changes his mind about me." Samantha grabbed Eddy's hand loosely and led him away from the villa.

As the three walked towards Samantha's villa, Jo filled him in on the details, omitting the fact that she knew who the man was. She knew that Eddy would never understand that she knew him and had let him get away. Samantha listened quietly and Jo hoped she wouldn't tell him the truth.

"If Jo had let me use my zip ties this case would be solved," Samantha said as Eddy's phone rang.

"I have to take this," he said apologetically as he walked away from the women.

"I got distracted," Jo muttered.

"You are never distracted," Samantha said. "You have never made a mistake in the past. You're not going to fool me into thinking that you did tonight."

"I'm sorry, I had to let him go," Jo explained.

"If he's the one that killed Valda and stole the necklace, why wouldn't we want him arrested?"

"He's not a killer." Jo frowned. "I know he's not. Besides why would he come back to the villa again? If he already has the necklace what's the point?"

"Maybe he wanted to finish the job." Samantha snapped her fingers. "Maybe he thought that Roger found out or saw too much. Maybe he was here to kill Roger."

"No way. One of the most important rules of theft is to never return to the scene. If you get away clean, stay away."

"I didn't realize crime had rules." Samantha looked at her. "Isn't there one about not turning on your fellow thief? Is that what happened here tonight, Jo? Did you really just let a murderer escape because you thought you owed him loyalty?"

"No," Jo said with conviction. "You don't understand. I let him go because we will get more information out of him if he's free than we will if he's in jail. We're not going to get anywhere near him to talk to him once he's locked up."

"And now you don't think he's off and running?" Samantha asked. "If he's smart he's headed for Mexico."

"No, I don't think he's running. He wants that necklace, he's wanted it for a long time. If there's any chance that it's still in play he won't stray far."

"Or maybe if there's any chance that he'll get a second chance with you?" Samantha smiled. "Don't you think, Jo?"

"Samantha, you have no idea what you're

talking about."

"Maybe not, but I do hope that you will tell me."

"Why do you have zip ties in your purse?" Eddy looked at Samantha as he walked back towards them.

"You never know when you might need to detain someone," Samantha replied.

"If you had told me you were going I might have been able to stop him," Eddy said.

"We can do some things by ourselves," Samantha said defensively.

"Let's all just try to get some sleep for now," Eddy said as he pushed his hat up off his forehead and scratched his head. "No more running off. We need to do this together or not at all." He looked from Samantha to Jo. "I'm not commanding, I'm requesting."

"I can agree to that." Jo nodded.

"Sounds good to me." Samantha walked off

towards her villa while Jo walked off towards hers. Eddy stood and watched them go, ever-vigilant.

Chapter Nine

Alone in her villa, Jo shed her clothes and changed into pajamas. She crawled into her bed with the hope that her exhaustion would slow down her thoughts. The moment her head hit the pillow, they began to race. They were filled with one person. Drew. In her wildest dreams she never thought she would run into Drew again. He was the type of man that a woman never forgot. But he was also the type of man that every woman tried their hardest to forget. He crawled into her heart and settled there, despite her protests. He made an impression on her that lasted a lifetime. Again, she reached up and touched her neck where the necklace should have been. Her eyes closed as her mind traveled back to the day he gave it to her.

"There's this necklace, called the 'Rose Diamond', it's sought after by every master thief. It's very valuable, and it would look perfect around your neck."

"Drew, you know I'm not interested in things like that."

"I know you say you're not. I also know that you deserve to have valuable things. Right now, this is the best I can offer. Consider it a place holder for the real deal, okay?" He held out the jewelry box to her. She opened it to find a silver necklace with a small rose charm. It was the first and last gift she received from a man. Though others tried, she always refused. Drew was the last man she allowed to crawl into her heart. Now he was back, not for her, but for that necklace that he was obsessed with.

As Jo began to fall asleep she thought about the sound of his voice, and the curve of his lips. Had she lied to Samantha when she said she let him go for the purpose of getting more information out of him? In the shadows of the room, as her heart slowed into a steady rhythm she wondered if he was capable of killing Valda. There was a time when he would do anything to get that necklace. Did that anything include murder?

***

Jo woke up still troubled by the thought that Drew could have killed Valda. She forced herself into the shower and then headed out to her garden. She always found peace with her hands in the dirt. There was a sense of freedom that came with giving life to plants. As she watered a few of her tomato plants she heard someone walk up to the garden. For just a second she hoped that it would be Drew. Instead it was Samantha.

"I heard from my contact. Tony Farie was paroled three months ago."

Jo dropped the hose. "Are you sure?"

"I'm sure, and not only that I saw him in the diner the other day," she said. "The day Valda was murdered."

"Really?" Jo said bewildered. "How did you know it was him?"

"I managed to get a picture of him and he has

this distinctive scar," Samantha said. "I'll never forget a scar like that. It is jagged and goes from the base of his hairline to his mouth."

"That seems like such a coincidence."

"I know." Samantha nodded. "I tried to get his last known address, but they couldn't access it."

"So, he was in the area on the day of the murder and there is a very good chance he's still here. There is an even better chance that he's going to go after Roger."

"The question is, does he have the necklace?" Samantha frowned. "We still don't know where it's ended up."

"No, we don't, but I can tell you that if it's anywhere nearby, Drew and Tony will stick around until it's found. If Roger somehow kept it, then he is in some serious danger."

"I think it's time we had a conversation with our friendly, new neighbor. We need to find out once and for all if he has that necklace," Samantha said.

"I agree," Jo said.

"But I'm not sure how we're going to do that."

Jo spun the bracelet on her wrist. "I think I can manage it. But we should meet with Eddy and Walt first to let them know what is going on."

"Yes, we'd better. Do you want to meet up at the café?"

"No, I have a better idea. Let's meet down by the water, in one of the gazebos. I want whoever might be watching us, whoever might be involved, to know that we are meeting and discussing them."

"Wow, I thought secrecy was your thing." Samantha said.

"Normally it is, but in this case a little creativity is going to be required. I think we need to draw them out. We have no idea where Tony is, or where Drew is. We have no idea where Roger might have stashed the necklace."

"I don't know if he would have had time to stash it. According to Walt and Eddy he was at the buffet most of the night."

"That's why I think it has to be in the house somewhere. If we hadn't been so rudely interrupted, we would have found out for sure." She clenched her jaw. "There's a good chance that Drew will do whatever it takes to get that necklace."

"Then we need to be extra cautious. You finish in your garden, just join us when you're done."

Jo nodded. She started to collect her gardening tools as Samantha walked away. She did her best not to feel it, but there was some disappointment within her that Drew hadn't bothered to come back in search of her. She did her best to push it out of her mind as she carried her tools to her shed. When she opened the door of the shed she was startled by the presence of a shadowy figure inside. She jumped back, poised to yell for help, but she was too late. He grabbed her by the arm and pulled her into the shed, then slammed the door shut.

Through the shadows Jo could see a very familiar body shape. Even after all of the years they were apart his shoulders and the slope of his neck were exactly the same. She drew long, slow breaths to try to slow down the pounding of her heart. Was he there to kill her?

"Drew, my friend is just outside."

"Your friend?" He smiled as he stepped closer to her. "No, your friend is already gone. Besides, is she really your friend if she knows nothing about you?"

"Samantha knows a lot more about me than anyone else. She wrote articles about me. She'll know that something is wrong if I don't show up to our meeting."

"Are you afraid of me, Jo?" Drew reached out and touched the curve of her cheek. "Really?"

"Shouldn't I be? You just pulled me into a dark shed."

"There was a time when that would have a different effect on you." He chuckled.

"A long time ago, Drew."

"Maybe, but time doesn't change everything, does it, Jo?"

"Why are you here?"

"You know why."

"I know, for the necklace. But why are you here, in my shed?" Jo queried.

"I'm here because you need to be more careful. You're lucky it was me that you caught breaking into Clem's place. It could have been someone else, and you would have faced some serious consequences."

"I'm lucky? I'm trying to enjoy my peace, my retirement, and you and your band of thieves are interfering with that."

"My band of thieves?" He laughed. "Okay if you want to put it that way, that's one perspective. But you're aware of how dangerous some of these thieves can be."

"Yes, I haven't forgotten that."

"So, you need to back off," Drew said earnestly.

"I don't understand why you are even still here?" She squinted to get a clearer view of his face. "Does Clem still have the necklace?"

"No one knows for sure. Most people think he does."

"And you? You know something, I can tell."

"I know Tony's out. I know he's been in the area. If anyone is going to have it, it will be him." He shrugged. "In a way it's rightfully his."

"Do you think he killed Clem's wife to get it?" Jo watched his eyes intently. Drew responded with an open gaze.

"I think it's possible. You still think I did it, don't you?"

"I don't know what to think. I did catch you breaking into Clem's house."

"And why would I do that if I already had the necklace?" He shook his head and sighed. "I wouldn't kill for anyone or anything, Jo, that hasn't changed. But some of these guys will, and if they think you might have the necklace, which they will once they discover who you are, they will come after you. That's why you have to stay out of this."

"Thanks for the advice." Jo locked her eyes to his. "I think you've said enough."

"Oh?" He stared at her for a moment and then nodded. "All right. But this belongs to you." He held out the necklace that she gave to Bucky. Jo watched it dangle between them for a moment.

"Are you going to take it? It belongs to you."

"I gave it to Bucky."

"I know you did. Now, I'm giving it back to you. Please, I want you to have it." He drew a slow breath. "I know that things will never be what they once were. But the memories have kept me company throughout the years, and I hope they've done the same for you." Jo took the necklace without saying a word. "I'm going, I'm going." He held up his hands. "But think about what I said, Jo. This is a dangerous game you're in the middle of."

Jo moved aside so that he could exit the shed. It took all of her strength to resist reaching for him. She had let him go once before, and with good reason. She knew that she had to let him go again. Once the door closed behind him, Jo looked down at the necklace. He was right, it did give rise to fond memories. She tucked it into her pocket to put away in her jewelry box later.

When Jo stepped out of the shed she decided to walk down to meet her friends. She wasn't ready to be alone in her villa. If Drew were to come back, she wasn't sure what she would do. The path to the gazebo was littered with leaves and grass shreds. Ahead of her she could see Samantha, Walt, and Eddy already at the gazebo. She wondered if she should tell them about her encounter with Drew.

"Jo, over here!" Samantha waved to her. Jo quickened her step. When she reached the gazebo

Eddy and Walt were deep in conversation.

"So, he's moved near here?" Walt asked.

"Yes, about twenty minutes away."

"Who?" Jo's heart skipped a beat as she guessed they were speaking about Drew.

"Tony," Eddy said. "I pulled some strings and I managed to get his address. He's just registered a new one with the parole board."

"Great! Then the police should be able to pick him up right now and all of this should be settled." Samantha sighed with relief.

"Wait, what about the necklace?" Jo looked between them. "If we have the police arrest Tony what if they don't recover the necklace? Plus we don't know if Tony and Clem were in on it together."

Eddy studied her. "Why would Clem work with Tony to kill Valda?"

"Why would Tony kill Valda if all he wanted was the necklace?" Jo raised an eyebrow. "Thieves aren't usually murderers."

"Maybe he was trying to get revenge." Samantha shrugged. "He wanted to take everything from Clem, not just the necklace, but his wife, too."

"I don't know." Jo shoved her hands in her pockets. "I'm just not convinced that Tony would kill her. Take the necklace, sure, but kill her?"

"Or maybe you just want to get your hands on that necklace?" Eddy smiled a little. "Old habits and all."

"All right, I do. But not for the reason that you think. If the police arrest Tony and don't recover the necklace, then Clem will still be in danger. Every skilled thief in the country will be after him to find the necklace, even if he doesn't have it. So, he will have lost his wife, and be hounded for the rest of his life. Does that seem like justice to you?"

"Maybe not, but neither does letting a murderer remain free. I mean Clem is still a thief." Eddy sat down on the edge of the picnic table and settled his gaze on her. "Do you want to tell me what this is really about?"

"It's really about the police not just going after the easy mark. That's who Roger, or Clem is."

"So, you don't think Clem did this, and you don't think Tony did this?" Samantha blinked. "Then who do you think did?"

Jo lowered her eyes. "I'm not sure. I'm not saying that neither of them did it, I just think that we should find out for sure before we go to the police."

"Well, there's one way to know if Tony has the necklace. We have his address now. Why don't we go take a look around?" Samantha looked over at Jo. "What do you think?"

"I guess it couldn't hurt. Maybe we'll find something that will give us a clue as to what really happened to Valda."

"I think it's also important not to forget that Clem hasn't reported the necklace stolen. He either has it, or he knows that someone stole it.

I'm sure he'll want to get it back if it's been taken." Walt stood up and strolled over to the edge of the gazebo. "I think we should be cautious in general."

"You're right. In fact, you should all know that some of the thieves that are looking for this necklace, will do just about anything to get it. Make sure you think through every choice you make, because they are smart and fast." Jo pursed her lips.

"It sounds like you have some familiarity with these people. Is that true, Jo?" Eddy frowned.

"Why?" Jo sighed.

"Listen Jo, I just hate to think of you being around people like that."

Jo's eyes widened with surprise. "Really?"

"So many thieves are always going to be looking for the easy road and what works to their advantage, if you're their friend or their enemy. Being surrounded by people like that can't be easy."

Jo twirled the charm on the necklace in her

pocket. Eddy was right. She was coming to realize that maybe Drew never truly cared about her. Maybe he cared more about what he could get from her.

"No, it wasn't." She smiled as she met Eddy's eyes. "I am much happier with the friends I have now."

"Good!" Samantha barreled towards her for a hug. When Jo pulled her hands out of her pockets to hug her in return she felt the necklace drop out of her pocket. Samantha hugged her so tight that she couldn't free herself right away. Walt leaned down and picked up the necklace.

"What's this?" He held up the necklace and met her eyes.

"It's nothing." She plucked the necklace from his hand. "Thanks." She held his gaze and hoped that he wouldn't tell the truth. It wasn't as if she really had anything to hide, but she didn't want to have to explain herself, especially to Eddy.

"All right, let's go if we're going." Eddy

clapped his hands together. Walt looked towards him and then nodded at Jo.

"While you guys are doing that I'll see if I can dig deeper into Valda's past. See if she had any enemies that wanted her dead," Walt said. "Maybe her murder had nothing to do with the necklace."

"And I will dig deeper with my resources. I want to know if Clem and Tony's relationship ended after Tony was arrested. I'll check to see if Clem has been to visit him at any time while he was in prison. I'll look into common associates as well. We should be able to turn up something. Just be careful, all right?" Samantha looked between Jo and Eddy. "Anyone that is willing to kill for a necklace is going to be willing to kill for freedom, too."

"We'll be careful." Eddy tilted his head towards the parking lot. "I'll drive?"

"Good. I just need to stop at my villa for a moment. Want to pick me up?" Jo asked.

"Okay." Eddy walked with Samantha back towards her villa. Walt lingered behind. As Jo started to walk away he cleared his throat.

"Jo. How did you get that necklace back? It's the same one that you gave to Bucky in exchange for information."

"I know that." Jo frowned. "Don't worry about it, Walt."

Walt sighed and pulled off his glasses. He brushed them against the front of his shirt then slid them back on. "I'm afraid I will, Jo. I mean, you're not the only one involved in all of this. We are all in knee deep now. Did you go back to see Bucky on your own?"

"No." Jo met his eyes. "It's not important right now."

"It is to me, Jo."

"I understand that, but I'm not sure it's a good idea to waste our time on this nonsense when we should be on our way to Tony's house to find out what he is up to." Jo tightened her lips. She knew that Walt wasn't easy to fool.

"Jo, I feel like you are holding something back here. I know that this must have ruffled some old feathers. But you must remember, no matter what old feelings are coming up for you now, you can still trust me. Me, and Eddy, and Samantha. Maybe these thieves, these criminals were your friends once, maybe you felt an obligation to be loyal to them, but things have changed. We're your friends now. We are the ones that you can trust, and I can assure you that we will be loyal to you. No matter what is going on, all you have to do is be open about it." He reached out and awkwardly touched her shoulder. "You're not on your own anymore, Jo."

Jo blinked back unexpected tears. They surprised her as they burned. Walt's words meant more to her than even she realized. Her heart fluttered with the notion of being open, completely open with someone.

"Okay Walt. Thank you."

He nodded.

She waited for him to demand more information, to insist that she reveal the truth, but he didn't. He only remained beside her, waiting. She reached into her pocket and pulled the necklace back out.

"When I started out as a cat burglar, I made a very big mistake, one that should have cost me my freedom, and even my life. A man, Drew, stepped in to help me. Not only did he protect me from the consequences, but he took me under his wing and taught me how not to get caught. He was a big part of my life. One day, he gave me this. It was special to me, because he didn't steal it. He went out and bought it. He had expensive jewelry at his fingertips, but he gave me something he had paid for. Anyway, not long after he gave me this, we went our separate ways."

"That's why Bucky called it a piece of history. True love between thieves." Walt smiled.

"I never said anything about true love." Jo

frowned.

"You didn't have to. It was in your voice, and in your eyes. It's okay, Jo. You're not going to fall to pieces by admitting that you were once vulnerable."

"Are you sure?" Jo smiled and fiddled with the charm on the necklace. "Whatever it was, it was over almost as fast as it started."

"Drew was the one who tried to break into Clem's?"

"Yes. I guess when he saw Bucky had this, he felt the need to give it back to me."

"That's sweet." Walt glanced over at the water. "I understand why you kept it to yourself. Eddy might not understand, and Samantha would probably try to get you two back together. But you should know, Jo, you can always be comfortable with me. One thing that numbers have taught me over the years is that there is no one without fault, there is no one as perfect as a mathematical calculation. We all have our moments, our mistakes, our miscalculations, they are what make us human instead of machines."

"Thanks Walt." Jo reached out and took his hand. Walt didn't pull his hand away from her, he let her hold it. She gave his hand a light squeeze before releasing it. "I better get going before Eddy sends out a search party. I really appreciate you listening."

"Anytime, Jo. Just remember, we can't be who we once were, no matter what. You can't go back."

"I know." Jo smiled sadly. "That much I know."

Chapter Ten

Jo left Walt at the gazebo and walked up the hill to her villa. She tucked her necklace safely into her jewelry box. It occurred to her that although expert thieves were swarming Sage Gardens and beyond in search of a priceless, antique necklace, Drew took the time to chase after what was worth little more than costume jewelry. She smiled to herself. Maybe she couldn't go back, but she could enjoy the moment. A knock on her door caught her attention.

"Jo, are you in there?"

"I'm here, Eddy, just one minute." She rushed to the door without a second thought about the necklace in her jewelry box. She had a more important one that she had to find.

"We're burning daylight." Eddy squinted at her when she opened the door.

"In my experience it's a bit easier to break into someone's house in the dark." Jo smiled as they walked to the car.

"Well, in my experience you're less likely to run into the home owner if you strike during work hours."

"Good point." Jo settled into the car and waited for Eddy to get in as well. "But in my experience, thieves, even retired ones, don't have day jobs."

"All right, you win." Eddy flashed her a grin. "Speaking of being retired, have you ever noticed that it's more exhausting than not being retired?"

Jo cringed. "Well, I don't have the best daily life to compare it to."

"I don't know, maybe I'm just restless. I find I spend most of my day trying to find things to keep myself occupied."

"You should start doing an activity."

"What? Like shuffleboard?" Eddy rolled his eyes.

"You, playing shuffleboard?" Jo laughed.

"That I'd like to see. No maybe something sporty."

"I can't do much, my knees and hips aren't what they used to be."

"Hm. Maybe a card game group?"

He glanced over at her. "I got thrown out of the last one. Something about my temper."

"Oh, really?" Jo pretended to be surprised and then laughed again.

"Hey, I'm a mild-mannered man."

"Eddy wait." Jo placed a hand on his arm as he was about to turn out of the driveway of Sage Gardens.

"What? Did you forget something?"

"No, I just think we're jumping the gun here."

"What do you mean?"

"Well, the person most likely to have that necklace is Roger, not Tony."

"But we didn't get very far with him."

"Like I told Samantha, I think we need to be a

little more creative."

"What are you thinking?" Eddy pulled off to the side of the driveway and looked over at her.

"As far as Roger knows I'm just another retiree. I doubt he has any clue about my history, or my connections."

"And?"

"And, if I let him know, if I confront him, not as myself, but as the person I used to be, then he might be willing to give me more information."

"Maybe, but that would also make you vulnerable. If the other thieves that are looking for this necklace find out that you live at Sage Gardens, you're going to become a target. No one is going to believe that a master thief practically living next door isn't involved when a priceless necklace goes missing."

"Aw." Jo smiled.

"Aw?" Eddy raised an eyebrow.

"You called me a master thief!"

"Oh, so that you consider a compliment?" He laughed. "All right, we can try it your way. But I'm going to be with you the entire time."

"No way, that will tip him off."

"I'm at least going to be close."

"Fine. You can be close. But Roger is not a danger to me, he just stumbled onto something valuable."

"Okay." Eddy turned the car around and drove towards Roger's house. He parked a few villas down. "I can see his car in the driveway."

"Like I said." Jo winked at him. "No day job."

"Just be careful, Jo. It's the people that we underestimate that can be the most dangerous."

Jo nodded and stepped out of the car. She made her way towards Roger's villa. She walked with a confidence and authority that she hadn't felt in a long time. Eddy followed after her, several steps back, at a casual pace. Jo walked up to the front door of the villa and knocked hard on it. There was no answer. She knocked again, so hard that the window beside the door rattled.

"What is it?" Roger threw the door wide open. His eyes widened when he saw Jo. "What are you doing here?"

"What's wrong, Roger? Are you having a bad day?"

"Yes. Of course I am. My wife is dead."

"Maybe I could come inside for a moment? We can talk about it."

Roger studied her. "What are you doing here?"

"Like I said, I just want to talk."

"I bet." He stepped aside and allowed her inside. Jo closed the door behind her.

"I guess you must not remember me. I don't think we ever met."

"We just met not that long ago." He narrowed his eyes. "Are you trying to play some kind of game here?"

"No. But I think you are, and you're losing,

and it's starting to get on my nerves."

"What are you talking about?" He balled his fists with impatience.

"I'm talking about the necklace, Roger. The necklace that you and I both know that you stole. Well actually, Tony stole it, but he landed in prison, didn't he?" He looked shocked that Jo knew so much.

"Yes." He frowned. "I don't have the necklace."

"Don't lie to me, Roger." Jo locked eyes with him. "I know a scam when I see one. You offed your wife and decided to keep the jewelry. Right?"

"Don't talk about her like that." Roger sniffed. "Who are you?"

"I'm someone who never would have let her partner be caught by the police. I'm someone who was once considered one of the best, not an amateur that stumbled into some good luck. I know what it's like to steal something that's worth a lot, and I know that's not something that you would give up so easily."

"I don't care. You don't know what you're talking about."

"I know that you didn't sell the necklace to the fence like you were supposed to."

"I couldn't. It was too hot. I didn't trust the fence not to turn me in or for it not to get back to me somehow. I've been stuck with that thing for so long, waiting to see when Tony would figure it out, or someone else would."

"I need to know where that necklace is, Roger."

"I don't know! I don't have it! How many times do I have to say it?"

"Maybe you don't understand me. I am not here because I want the necklace. I am not here because I care that you are a thief, or even that you may have killed your wife. I am here because I was once a thief, and all of the thieves that you have drawn out with your reckless behavior will think that I am somehow involved in this. They are not going to leave me alone until they have that necklace. So, as long as you are hiding that necklace, I am going to be in danger. There's only two ways to solve that problem. Either you tell me where you're hiding the necklace, or you tell me who took it."

"Stop it!" Roger pleaded. "I don't have it. If I had it, do you think that I would still be here? They're hunting me, too."

"So, where is it?"

"It has to be Tony. He's the only one that would have known I'd still have it after all these years and he would have wanted it back."

"You think he killed your wife?"

"I don't know." Roger shook his head. "I've never thought of Tony as a murderer. But they say prison changes a person."

"So, you suspect that Tony robbed you and murdered your wife, but you haven't told the police?" Jo raised her eyebrows.

"Oh yes that would work out well for me.

Excuse me officer, not only do I think my wife was murdered, but I believe that the guy I robbed a wealthy family with several decades ago, is the one who did it. Oh, and by the way, he stole the necklace we originally stole. How fast do you think I would be behind bars if I told them that?"

"I can see that you're real broken up about your wife's death." Jo crossed her arms.

"Don't do that. That's not fair. I loved my wife. What am I supposed to do with people hunting me? All I can think is when will I be next?"

"There's a way to fix that, Roger, by turning yourself in. The police are not even investigating this as a crime."

"I can't do that. I just can't. Prison changes a person."

"Right." Jo nodded. She knew all too well how prison can change a person. "If you really don't have the necklace then you need to let me know if you find out for sure who does. Understand?"

"Yes, all right, I understand."

"Good." Jo turned and walked back out the door. As she started down the driveway she was startled by movement out of the corner of her eye. "Eddy, don't sneak up on me."

"I was watching through the window. Do you think he has the necklace?"

"No. I don't." She shook her head.

"Then you don't think he killed his wife?" Eddy led her towards the car.

"I don't know what to think about that. But Tony should be our main suspect when it comes to the robbery." She bit her lip to keep from adding that Drew was a possibility, too. "The only way to know for sure is if we go take a look around Tony's house. I'm almost completely convinced that Roger doesn't have the necklace, so Tony is the next best option on the list."

"All right, back to plan A."

Chapter Eleven

The drive to Tony's house took much longer than it needed to. Not only was it hampered by traffic, but Eddy got lost as well, even though he wouldn't admit it to Jo. Jo was too preoccupied to notice as she glanced in the windows of the cars that passed them. She expected to see a familiar face at any moment. It was hard for her to relax. She felt on edge. She felt like she was being followed. If she had that feeling it never failed to turn out to be true. Eddy noticed her searching gaze.

"What's wrong?"

"Nothing. I don't know." Jo shook her head. "I just feel like someone is following us."

Eddy glanced in the rearview mirror. "I'm pretty sure that I'd notice that."

Jo nodded, but continued to look out the window.

"Here it is." Eddy parked the car and looked through the window at the small house. It wasn't much to look at, but it was quite tidy and clean. "Looks like someone has been weeding and mowing."

"Looks like it." Jo popped her door open. She squinted as she looked up and down the street. "Quiet area."

"At least it looks quiet." Eddy stepped up beside her. "Do you think Tony is home?"

"No car in the driveway. There's a good chance he isn't."

"Pity, I guess we won't get a chance to question him."

"No, but I can take a look around."

"If that's what you want to do, I'll keep a lookout." Eddy nodded.

Jo smiled. Eddy once disliked the idea of her breaking into places, he had certainly softened to the idea. She walked around the side of the house to find a good window to crawl through. She wasn't the only one who had that idea, it seemed. She spotted two legs sticking out of one of the windows.

"Oh Drew." She sighed and shook her head. She knew that Eddy wasn't going to let Drew slide. In fact, he might even implicate Drew in the murder. The person started edging his way down from the window. Jo grabbed one of the feet sticking out the window and tugged hard. There was a flurry of movement, then Jo found herself staring down the barrel of a gun. The man who held it was not Drew at all.

"Roger! Or should I say Clem?" Jo scowled at him. "Put that gun down right this second!"

"What are you doing here?" He stared at her with wide eyes. "Why are you here?"

"I'm here to find out if your old friend, Tony, killed your wife, or perhaps it was you after all. You gave me a good sob story, but this doesn't look like the actions of a grieving widower."

"You keep quiet, you have no idea what you're

talking about."

"No? I know this is Tony's house. Did he ask you to break in? Or was that just your way of being a good friend? Maybe make up for the fact that you bilked him out of all of the money he would have made on that necklace you stole together?"

"Oh, you know far too much, don't you?" He released the safety on his gun and pointed it more directly at her face. "I guess that you think you know everything. I don't care why you are involved in this, but I don't need some nosy neighbor getting in the middle of my business."

Jo thought of Eddy at the front of the house. As long as all was quiet out there she knew that he wouldn't come looking for her. If she called out to him, Clem might kill her on the spot and then kill Eddy.

"You know what I don't understand, Clem?"

"It's Roger, call me Roger."

"Okay, Roger. You know what I don't understand? Valda. She didn't have to die. All of this was about the necklace, wasn't it? So why did anyone have to die?"

"Keep quiet."

"I mean it, Roger. Do you think of her? I mean, you must have loved her. Why else would you let her wear your most prized possession? You had to know that it was a risk for her to even know about it, let alone wear it."

"Of course I loved her, she was my wife! Why do you think I'm here?"

"For the necklace."

"Yes." He growled and started to lower the gun. "But not for the reasons that you think. I'm here because she loved that necklace. It took her from me, and I want her to go to her grave wearing it."

"I don't believe you. You plan to put a priceless piece of jewelry into a coffin?"

"Yes, I do. I will make sure that no more blood is shed over it."

"Did you find it?" Jo met his eyes. "Did Tony have it?"

"No, I didn't find it." Roger lowered his eyes. "I heard your car and I thought it was Tony. I didn't get a chance to finish my search."

"That's a shame." Jo flicked her eyes from Roger to the house. She wondered if there was some way to warn Eddy.

"Now, I'm going to have to get rid of you." Roger sighed.

"Listen, I was once one of the best thieves around. I promise you if that necklace is inside that house I will be able to find it. So, you can either wave that gun around like you're going to hurt me and waste both of our time, or I can go in and have a look around before Tony gets back."

"That sounds like an offer to work together." Roger smiled.

"No, it's not. It's an offer to help you find out who murdered your wife. You only get one chance to accept it. If you don't, then I will take that gun from you and make sure that you never see the outside of a prison cell again. It's your choice, Roger."

Roger lowered his gun. He stared hard at her. "You really think you're tough don't you?"

"I guess we'll just have to find out. Won't we?" She grabbed the edge of the window. Jo was very aware that at any moment Roger could choose to use the gun. She was fully exposed to him. But she didn't think he would. She knew that he wanted the necklace more than he wanted her dead.

Jo jumped down through the window and found herself in the middle of a pile of trash. She scrunched up her nose at the smell in the house. It was clear that Tony hadn't learned good hygiene while in prison. Still, she focused on the hunt for the necklace. There were two things weighing on her mind. One, she knew that Tony would be aware many thieves would be hunting the necklace, so he would hide it somewhere clever. Two, she didn't have a lot of time before either Tony came home or Roger started shooting.

She didn't believe he was violent, but people had surprised her many times before.

Jo made her way from the living room into the back bedroom. After a quick glance around the room she ruled out several obvious places. There was a safe in the closet, a lockbox on the dresser, and the mattress was off kilter. All of these places were the first places a thief would look. However, the mattress being out of place brought her attention to the curtain rod that ran the length of the window above the bed. The house was messy, the bed wasn't made, and Tony had paid absolutely no attention to design. However, the curtain rod was brand new, thick, without a trace of dust on it. When she climbed on top of the bed to reach it, the mattress shifted.

The rod was smudged with fingerprints. Jo smiled with triumph as she lifted the rod down. It wasn't as heavy as she expected. She unscrewed the cap at one end and tipped up the other end. She held her hand out and waited for the necklace to slide down into her palm. After a few seconds she realized that wasn't happening. She did her best to peer into the curtain rod. It was hard to see inside. With the curtain rod balanced in one hand she reached into her pocket for her keys with her other hand. On her key chain she had a penlight which she shone into the curtain rod. There was not a trace of the necklace, or anything else for that matter, inside the rod. Jo's heart dropped. She was so certain that she had found the hiding spot, but she was wrong. Just like she had been wrong about being followed. Maybe her instincts were rusty, or completely broken.

She placed the curtain rod back on the hooks just as she heard a crash outside. It was followed by an assortment of very colorful language. Jo raced back to the window she had climbed in through. As she started to climb back through it, she caught sight of the front door. It wasn't closed all the way. If Roger broke in the front door, why did she catch him climbing out the window? Maybe he saw her out front and decided to exit a different way.

Jo jumped down from the window and nearly landed on top of Eddy and Roger. The two men wrestled on the ground with grunts and curses.

"Eddy! Let go of him!"

"He has a gun!" Eddy growled.

"I'm not going to use it!" Roger placed the gun on the ground. Jo reached down and scooped it up.

"There, now both of you stop! We need to figure out what is happening here!" Jo said.

Eddy glowered at Roger as he got to his feet. "What is going on is that he was waiting out here for you with a gun. He clearly killed his wife and was prepared to do the same to you."

"I think you're wrong about that, Eddy. I knew he was here, and I knew he had a gun, before I ever went in."

"What?" Eddy's eyes widened. "Why would you do something so reckless?"

"We're all looking for the same thing," Jo said.

"A murderer?" Eddy's eyes flashed. "Because that's what I'm looking for."

"The only way we are going to find the murderer is if we find the necklace."

"You didn't find it?" Roger looked at her with some disappointment.

"I thought I had. I really did. It was the perfect hiding spot. But it wasn't there." She shook her head.

"We need to get out of here before Tony comes back." Eddy grimaced.

"Wait, we should shut the front door first or he will know that someone was here."

"Why did you open it?" Roger rolled his eyes. "You had time to do that, but not find the necklace?"

"Excuse me, but I was distracted by the two of you out here wrestling like teenage boys."

"He had a gun!" Eddy waved his hands with exasperation.

"So? Who doesn't have a gun?" Roger said.

"Wait a minute." Jo narrowed her eyes. "Are you saying that you didn't open the front door, Roger?"

"No. I didn't. Why would I go in the front door and risk being seen? I'm not that stupid."

Jo didn't argue, but she knew that going in the front door wasn't stupid at all. Drew taught her from the first day that the best way not to get caught was to act as if you belonged there. Walk up to the front door, use your body to shield whatever tool you're using to break in, and to anyone passing by it will appear that you are just unlocking the door.

"Maybe Tony took off suddenly for some reason," Roger said.

"Whatever the reason might be we should get out of here," Eddy said.

"You're right, let's go." Jo hurried towards the car. Roger went off in a different direction when they reached the sidewalk.

"Get in, get in." Eddy unlocked the doors. Jo jumped into the passenger seat and Eddy started the car the moment he was inside. "We should be arresting him."

"Well remember, you're not a cop, and I don't have handcuffs."

"I know." Eddy drove down the road with his hands curled around the steering wheel so tight that his knuckles turned white. "I can't believe that you did that."

"It was a judgment call, Eddy. He had a gun."

"You could have called for me."

"And then he might have shot us both. I thought it would be safer to go inside. I wanted to search the place anyway."

"Did you find anything?"

Jo sighed. "I thought I did. But it turned out to be nothing. I don't know, Eddy, we keep hitting up against brick walls."

"It's a bit complicated. It's almost like Valda's

death is an afterthought. Samantha called while you were in there Walt did some searching on Valda and he couldn't find anyone in her past that had anything against her. I still think she was just an innocent bystander at the time of the crime. It's hard to figure out who would be so vicious, when she doesn't have any personal enemies that we can find. It looks like she wasn't the target, the necklace was, she just got in the way."

"Are we sure about that?" Jo rested her head against her fist and looked over at Eddy. "Maybe we zeroed in so much on the necklace that we overlooked a simpler answer. Maybe she was the target. Anyone who killed her would have taken the necklace, too. Nobody leaves a piece of jewelry like that behind. Let's not forget that Roger was angry at her for wearing the necklace to the front door. He might have lost his temper with her and thought she was too big of a risk of exposing him."

"Roger was at the buffet though." Eddy shook his head. "I really don't think that he would have had time to get from the buffet, to Valda, lose his temper with her, kill her, and then stash the necklace, all while leaving no evidence behind."

"You're right, that is pretty farfetched, but it might be possible. Maybe he killed her before he went to the buffet and pretended to find the body afterwards."

"That's possible." Eddy nodded thoughtfully. "I'll get Samantha to see if she can find out a more accurate time of death."

"I think it is still possible that someone out of the blue broke in and attacked her," Jo said.

"Now you're thinking that someone random might have killed her?" Eddy asked.

Jo pursed her lips. She gazed out through the windshield. It was grasping at straws to think that the necklace wasn't the target. The truth was, with Roger getting lower on the list of suspects, it was getting much harder to believe that Drew was innocent.

"Samantha also said that she couldn't find any evidence that Tony and Roger have had any contact with each other since Tony was arrested."

"Interesting," Jo said. "Another dead end."

"Let's get everyone together at my place and we'll regroup. I think you could use a break, Jo. When was the last time you ate?"

Jo waved her hand without concern. "I'm not sure."

"Then we need to get some food in your stomach. Jo, you can't let these things consume you. Trust me, I know from experience. If you stop taking care of yourself you'll never solve the crime."

"It's nice to know that you're concerned."

"Why wouldn't I be?"

Jo stole a glance at him and smiled. "Thanks Eddy. I'll go ahead and text Samantha and Walt to meet us there."

"Perfect." Eddy nodded.

Chapter Twelve

When Eddy and Jo arrived at Eddy's villa, Samantha and Walt were already there.

"So, no luck?" Walt stepped back to let Eddy unlock the door.

"All we did was run into Roger breaking into Tony's house to get the necklace back." Eddy shook his head.

"But we didn't find the necklace." Jo frowned.

"Well, that just means we have another chance to look for it." Samantha smiled. "I have to say that I'm rather enjoying the hunt." The eyes of all the others turned on her. Jo raised an eyebrow. "What?" Samantha shrugged. "We're essentially hunting for lost treasure. That doesn't seem like fun to any of you?"

"Maybe it would be fun if we had a solid clue about where to look." Jo frowned. "I am the most experienced treasure hunter out of all of us, but I can't get it right. My instincts are going haywire."

"Oh, trust me." Eddy clapped her lightly on the shoulder. "That's called old age."

"Speak for yourself." Samantha raised an eyebrow. "Jo, maybe you just need some rest."

"Maybe." Jo nodded and joined the others as they entered the villa.

"I found out that the estimated time of death was around ten," Samantha said. "Shortly before the body was found by Roger."

"So that rules out Roger again because he was at the buffet," Eddy said. "He couldn't have murdered her before going there."

Jo settled on one side of the couch. Eddy pressed a drink into her hand, a few minutes later Samantha presented a sandwich. Jo couldn't focus on what was being said or done. She heard snippets of conversation about Valda's body, the absence of any trouble from Valda's past, and their inability to locate the necklace. But what really occupied her mind was that the front door was left open. As much as she wanted to believe that Tony might have been in the house, she was almost certain that someone else was there.

"Jo, can I talk to you?" Samantha sat down next to her. Jo nodded and looked over at her. Samantha waited until Eddy and Walt were engaged in an argument over the justice system versus rehabilitation, then she scooted closer to Jo on the couch and lowered her voice.

"While I was going around in circles I did a little research on Drew. I hope you don't mind."

"What kind of research?"

"Well, I know the two of you have been out of touch for a very long time, so I just wanted to look into what he's been up to."

"Oh." Jo frowned. "What did you find?"

"It isn't good." Samantha lowered her voice even further, to a whisper. "There have been two charges of assault, but he was not prosecuted on either one."

"Well, then he probably didn't do it."

"Maybe. Or he might have cut a deal of some kind, or there wasn't enough evidence to hold him."

"He's not violent, but knowing Drew, even if he punched a police officer in the face he would find his way out of it. He's highly intelligent and very charismatic."

"Which makes him even more dangerous."

"Samantha?" Jo leaned towards her.

"Listen, I've done my best to hold my tongue on this, but I don't want you to be at risk. Whoever you thought Drew was all those years ago, you don't know if he still is."

Jo grimaced. "I know that. I'm not so foolish to think that I can trust him. I don't think he's a murderer, but lately my instincts have all been wrong."

"I don't think that they're wrong. There are a ton of emotions involved in all of this for you, Jo. I'm sure you're just having a hard time sorting through them to get to the truth. But in time you will figure it out. Until then, I just want to make sure that you use caution around Drew. I have instincts, too, and Drew strikes me as someone who will do whatever it takes to get whatever it is that he wants."

"You're right about that." Jo sighed. "I think I need some air." As she walked out of the villa she passed through Eddy and Walt's heated conversation.

"You can't throw a person away based on a mistake," Walt insisted.

"Some mistakes you can't come back from," Eddy argued.

Jo closed her eyes and closed the door behind her. Had Drew made a mistake that he couldn't come back from? She hated to think it, but she knew that it was possible.

Jo stood outside the door and stared into the distance. It kept bothering her that the front door of Tony's house was open. Had he been there when they arrived? Was that why the necklace was gone? She shifted from foot to foot. He might have hidden it somewhere, but where? The curtain rod seemed like the perfect place. Despite her breaking in they were no closer to knowing who had the necklace or who murdered Valda. It made her uneasy to think that maybe Tony somehow knew she was on her way there and had taken the time to grab the necklace before bolting out the door. Or perhaps, her instincts were wrong and the necklace was never in the curtain rod. What they needed was a way to draw Tony into admitting that he had the necklace.

Jo bit into her bottom lip and closed her eyes. She ran through memories of different break-ins she had taken part in. Then she recalled one particular event. Drew wanted to steal a particular collectible, but it was already stolen. No one knew who had it. He decided to set a trap by baiting other thieves with the idea that he had the item. He leaked to them that it was in a particular place. Then he sat outside and watched as one by one all of the thieves attempted to find it. All except one.

He knew then, the one who had not attempted to get it, was the one who had it all along. As far as she knew he never successfully stole the item, but he did find out who had it.

"Eddy?" Jo poked her head inside the villa. "I have an idea."

"What is it?" Eddy stood up and walked over to her.

"You're not going to like it." Jo eyed him hesitantly.

"Why not?"

"Because we're going to need Roger's help to pull off what I'm planning."

"What?" He frowned. "That man is not trustworthy. I'm not convinced that he didn't have a part in the necklace going missing and the murder. He's one of our suspects. How can we work with him to find out who the killer is if it might be him?"

"I'm not convinced that he's innocent either, but we need to make him think that we believe him, that way he will cooperate with us. In the long run it will pay off. I want to set a trap. I want to tell Roger that we believe that he doesn't have the necklace, but that we're going to pretend that he does to get Tony or whoever else might be interested in the necklace to come looking for it." She lowered her eyes as she wondered if Drew would be one of them. She couldn't worry about that, as she knew that she had to focus on solving the crime, not protecting Drew. "So, we'll tempt them and then wait for them to show up. If Tony doesn't show, then we'll know he has it."

"What if Roger has it?" Eddy asked.

"I don't think he does, but even if he does, he'll play along, he's not going to admit to having it, right?"

"Right, he probably won't." Eddy nodded.

"And if he does admit to it then we'll at least know that he has it," Jo said.

"So, if Tony does show up, we'll know Tony doesn't have it, and we don't have to focus on him."

"We can set up the sting at Roger's place. That will probably give me time to do a thorough search of his house. I believe that if Roger has the necklace it will be somewhere in the house," Jo stated.

"All right." Eddy ran his hand back through his hair."

"I'll leak the information to my contact so it can get back to Tony," Jo said.

"Good. We can have Walt monitor Tony's movements to see if he goes anywhere. If he does have the necklace and someone else claims to have it, I guarantee you he'll go to wherever he is hiding it to check to make sure that it is still there."

"Good point." Jo smiled. "I like the way you think, Eddy."

"I think you're the only one." Eddy grinned.

As the two began to work out the plan for the sting the next day Walt and Samantha joined in.

"You do realize that you'll be the target of anyone who wants this necklace right?" Walt sighed. "I'm not so sure that's the best idea."

"Maybe not, but it's the only one we have right now." Jo frowned. "The longer we let this go on, the more likely it is that Valda's death will get swept under the rug."

"She's right." Samantha nodded. "At this point there is no evidence that we know of to prove who killed her. Maybe if we find out who has the necklace it will lead us to the murderer or even a confession."

"I hope so." Eddy yawned. "But before we do any of that, we all need some rest. Jo and I will head to Roger's in the morning. Let's all plan to get into position by eight, that way we can catch Roger and Tony before either of them think about leaving the house."

"Good plan." Samantha nodded. "I'll do a little more research tonight, too. I want to know if there is anything floating around on the internet about the necklace."

"I'm going to head home." Jo stepped out of the villa. Walt stepped out behind her.

"I'll walk you."

"That's not necessary."

"I know, but I could use the company." Walt smiled. Jo thought about arguing, but she decided against it. If she was honest with herself she felt like company. The two began to walk in silence towards Jo's villa. After a few minutes, Walt took a short breath and looked over at her.

"Are you doing okay?"

"Why wouldn't I be?"

"Drew."

Jo blinked. "I thought we agreed not to mention that?"

"I agreed not to mention it to anyone else. I never agreed not to make sure that you're okay."

"I'm fine."

"Even after seeing him again?"

"Yes, whatever we had ended a very long time ago." Jo paused at the end of her walkway. "I appreciate your concern, Walt, I really do. But I've never been the romantic type. I wasn't then, and I'm not now. Sure, at one time Drew and I were close, but we're entirely different people now. I don't want anyone to get the impression that I am somehow still involved with him."

"I didn't mean it that way, Jo. Of course I know you're not."

"You might know that, but I doubt that Eddy will see it that way. I'd just prefer to pretend there is no connection between us. All right?" Jo met his eyes. "Please?"

"Sure." He nodded. "I have no problem with that. But will you be able to say the same if he turns out to be responsible for Valda's death? You know that you don't owe this man anything, right?"

Jo clenched her jaw. "If Drew is the one who killed Valda, trust me I will be the first person to make sure that he pays for it."

"All right." Walt rocked back on his heels and nodded. "Good night, Jo."

"Good night, Walt." She walked up to her villa and closed the door behind her. She hoped that Walt believed her. More than that, she hoped that she would be able to live up to her own words.

Chapter Thirteen

Bright and early the next morning Jo found Eddy waiting on her doorstep.

"Are Samantha and Walt in place?" Jo asked.

"Samantha is getting ready to keep an eye on Roger's place and Walt is already sitting on Tony's house."

"Great." Jo nodded. "Well, I guess it's time to see if we can get Roger to cooperate with us."

"I thought it would be better if we walked. That way there are no extra cars around Roger's villa to make it look suspicious."

"Good idea."

"Jo, I'm going to ask you something, but I don't want you to be offended by the question," Eddy said as they walked towards Roger's villa.

"All right." Jo looked over at him. "What is it?"

"Do you think that any of your old friends

have realized you live here in Sage Gardens?"

Jo thought about the fact that Drew knew. "Not anyone that we need to be concerned about."

"That's a rather evasive answer." Eddy quirked a brow.

"Well, it was a rather invasive question. I have no idea who might know where I live. I've done my best to keep a low profile, but those I knew in the past could find anything that they were looking for, including people."

"I understand that." Eddy frowned.

"Then why ask the question?" Jo shrugged. "I don't know anything more than you know, unless you're insinuating that I'm in contact with some of these people."

"I didn't say that. I asked you not to get offended, remember?"

"Oh right, sorry." She sighed and paused at the walkway that led up to Roger's house. "Are we doing this or not?"

"We are," Eddy said. "I didn't mean to upset you, Jo."

"Don't worry about me, worry about Valda." Jo walked up towards the front door of Roger's house. Eddy followed after her. Jo knocked on the door. After a few minutes Roger opened it. He stared at Jo and then at Eddy.

"I wasn't sure whether to answer. I thought you might have the police with you."

"I kind of do." Jo offered a half-smile. "Eddy is retired police."

"Great." Roger shook his head. "What do you want from me?"

"The same thing that you want, Roger. We want to solve Valda's murder."

Roger stuck his head out the door and looked up and down the street before looking back at Jo.

"Careful what you say."

"Why?" Jo raised an eyebrow. "Are you expecting someone?"

"No."

"Well, you might have a few guests soon. We're going to tell the criminal world that you have the necklace." Eddy smiled. "Soon, everyone who wants that necklace will be headed for this villa."

"Are you kidding me?" He stared at Eddy and Jo. "There's no way I'm going to tell anyone that I have the necklace. They'll come after me, they'll slaughter me."

"Don't worry, Roger, I'll be here to protect you." Jo flashed him a bright smile. "Are you going to let me stay? Because we've already exposed you and spread the rumor. So, either you stay here all by yourself, or you stay here with Eddy and me to look out for you. Which is it going to be?"

"All right, all right," he growled. "I can't believe you put me in the middle of all of this."

"Actually you're the one that did that to yourself, when you stole the necklace in the first place." Eddy shook his head. "If I were you, and I lost my wife, I'd be willing to do whatever it takes to find her killer."

"Enough of the guilt trips, will you just get in here?"

Jo surveyed the interior of the villa. She noticed that the place hadn't changed much since the first time she was there. She casually looked for anything that might be out of place, such as a statue in a new spot, or books on the bookshelf shuffled around. There wasn't much for her to see. Eddy began checking the windows of the villa.

"We want to make sure that everything is secure so that we don't have any surprises."

"Am I supposed to offer you drinks?" Roger frowned as he stood near the entrance of the kitchen. "This is the strangest party I've ever hosted."

"Roger, we're here to help you, a drink wouldn't hurt." Jo smiled.

"I'll see what I can do."

Once Roger was in the kitchen, Jo grabbed Eddy by the elbow. "Do you have contact with Walt?"

"Yes, he's texting me his every movement." Eddy squinted at his phone. "Apparently he just disinfected his phone and is horrified by what came off it."

"Great." Jo tried not to laugh. "Any news on Tony?"

"He hasn't seen any movement."

Jo's eyes flicked to the window. Would Drew find out and take the bait?

"And Samantha?"

"She's got her finger on the pulse of all of the police movement in the area, and she is driving around the block to spot any incoming vehicles or anyone on foot. We should have a good amount of notice before anyone tries to break in."

"Maybe this wasn't such a great idea." Jo wrung her hands nervously. "We're putting Roger in danger."

"I don't mind." Roger returned with two glasses of water. "I just want this to be over."

Jo took her glass. Eddy took his as well.

"We're all working towards the same goal then." Eddy nodded. Jo went to take a sip of her water, but stopped when Eddy gave her a slight shake of his head. Jo nodded. Roger turned on the television and sat down on the couch.

"I'm just going to use the bathroom." Jo set her glass down.

"Feel free. You can look in the toilet tank and under the rug, you're not going to find it. I told you I don't have it." Roger shrugged.

"I didn't say you did," Jo said.

"I'm not stupid. I know that you want to search the place. Go ahead and tear it apart. All you'll find are boxes waiting to be unpacked and memories of my wife that I can't even look at." Roger sniffled. Eddy frowned.

"I'm sorry this must be hard for you." He sat down beside Roger. "I bet she loved that necklace."

"Of course she did, it was the only nice thing that I could offer her. I never had anything else. She was the one that had some money. I couldn't get any good job, I wasn't actually a good thief, I just did that one job. I would have been a millionaire if I had been able to sell that necklace, but I couldn't. It was too recognizable and I knew that whoever saw it would know what it was. The one thing I could give her was that necklace. And that's what got her killed." He put his head in his hands. "I wish I'd never listened to Tony. If I had just refused to get involved, none of this would have ever happened."

Jo studied him with sympathy. His story echoed her own feelings about how she got caught up in being a cat burglar. It was easy to get into, and very difficult to escape. If it wasn't for prison, she might never have found a new life.

"But you didn't refuse." Eddy looked over at him. "You went ahead and did whatever Tony told you to do, and you haven't paid the price for that."

"Isn't my wife a price?" Roger looked up at him. "She's gone, isn't she?"

"Yes." Jo sighed. "This discussion isn't going to help matters. It's just going to distract us."

"You're right." Eddy nodded. "Roger, why don't you see if you can find us something to watch?" Eddy gestured towards the television. Jo moved closer to Eddy and whispered in his ear.

"I'm going to take a quick look around. Keep Roger distracted."

"All right, I will, but be careful, Jo. Who knows what he might have hidden in one of those boxes."

"He seems like a run of the mill guy."

"A run of the mill guy who once had in his possession one of the most expensive pieces of jewelry in this country. That makes him someone who might have a few secrets. Don't you think?"

"I do." Jo nodded. She looked over at Roger as he fought with his television.

"I knew they didn't set up the damn cable right. I told the guy he wasn't doing it right. He didn't want to listen. Now it's going to be ten business days before anyone else will come back out."

While he griped Jo slipped down the hallway towards the back bedroom. As she walked the heel of her boot got caught on the edge of the carpet. She looked down to see that the carpet was pulled back from the wall. She crouched down beside it and took a closer look. With a finger hooked under the surface of the carpet she tugged it back further from the wall. Tucked far beneath the carpet was a thin envelope. Jo glanced up and back towards the living room to ensure that Roger was still occupied with the television. He had just settled down onto the couch. She pulled the envelope carefully and quietly out from under the carpet. It wasn't sealed. She opened the envelope. Inside were several hundred dollar bills. There wasn't a large amount of money, maybe a few thousand, but someone valued it enough to pull back the carpet and hide it underneath.

Was it Roger's or Valda's stash or did it belong to both of them? If it was Valda's stash then maybe she was not only hiding it from robbers, but from her husband. Maybe she wanted to have some 'run away' money, which meant she was not as happy as she seemed. Maybe because of Roger's strange behavior of not allowing her to wear her necklace outside of the house. Maybe there were other issues in the marriage that were hidden beneath the surface, just as the stash of money had been. Jo slid the envelope back under the carpet. She knew that asking Roger about it wouldn't help anything.

When she stood back up she pushed through the bedroom door. The bed wasn't made. There were a few boxes in the closet. On one side of the bed a lamp stood bare of any shade. It was clear that Valda hadn't added her touch to the room just yet. She started inspecting the areas she could see. There was nothing on top of the dresser or on the shelves that drew her interest. When she looked under the bed she noticed that all of Roger's shoes were lined up nice and neat.

On the other side of the bed all of Valda's shoes were lined up in the same way. She had taken the time to make sure they had what they needed exactly where she thought it should be, so maybe she wasn't on the way out the door straight away. Maybe she had gotten wind of Roger's past and wanted to make sure that they had a back-up plan. Or maybe she simply knew that her husband didn't have much and she was saving for them.

Jo opened the drawers of the dresser. Inside the top right drawer was a pile of assorted socks. They were neat and tidy as well. It was clear that Valda liked things to be neat and tidy. If she found out about Roger's past, everything would have gotten very messy. So far the only sign that she might have known was the hidden money. Jo couldn't be sure if that was even Valda's money. She sighed and sat down on the end of the bed. There wasn't much to find in the bedroom, it was another dead end. It seemed this entire case was a series of dead ends. She did her best to refocus. She didn't think it would take very long for word to get out that Roger had the necklace. Once it did she hoped they would be able to get a lead. Until then, she could question Roger and hope that he told her the truth.

Jo started to walk back into the living room when she noticed Roger's phone on the kitchen table. She paused and glanced towards him. He was still occupied with Eddy and the television. She picked up his phone and checked to see if it had a password. The screen went straight into recent calls. She skimmed through the numbers on the phone. She noticed that there was one call that came in on the night of the murder at eleven minutes past ten, so around the estimated time of death. She looked at the information and saw that the call lasted three minutes and six seconds. There was no name, only a phone number. She pulled out her phone and quickly dialed the number, both so that it would be saved in her phone, and to see who it belonged to. A voicemail picked up, but it was a recording that only stated the phone number. She hung up and dialed Samantha.

"Nothing yet." Samantha didn't even bother to greet her. "I've seen a lot of people walking dogs, but no one that looked like a thief."

"They don't wear signs around their neck."

"Okay, I know that." Samantha cleared her throat. "No need to be rude."

"I'm sorry, I didn't mean to be snappy. Do you think you can find out who a phone number belongs to?"

"It should be fairly simple. What's the number?"

"I'll text it to you." Jo hung up the phone and quickly texted the number to Samantha. Samantha texted back.

Got it. Will update you when I find out.

Jo carefully put the phone back down on the counter. Her suspicion of Roger had waned, but this brought it right back to the surface. Maybe he was at the buffet, but knew exactly what was happening at his villa. Maybe he hired someone to do the job, and they called to let him know that it was done. The money under the carpet could have even been payment to the assassin. It was possible that the murderer ran without looking for the payment because he was spooked by someone or something.

Jo lingered near the kitchen and waited to hear from Samantha. She knew it might take some time for her to find out who the owner of the number was. As the minutes slid by her stomach knotted tighter and tighter. She could only hope that Samantha would find something before she couldn't hold back any longer and demanded to know the truth from Roger. She kept her eye on the phone screen as she still had her phone on silent. A few minutes later Samantha called. Jo stepped through the kitchen and out the back door before she answered.

"What did you find?"

"I found out that number belongs to our recently liberated friend, Tony."

"So, Tony and Roger spoke at the time of Valda's death for about three minutes?" Jo frowned.

"That seems to be the case."

"All along, they must have planned the whole thing together."

"That's one possibility."

"Well, it's time I found out the truth." Jo hung up the phone.

Chapter Fourteen

Now that Jo knew that Roger and Tony had spoken around the time of Valda's murder she was furious. She stormed back into the villa. Eddy and Roger looked over at her, both startled by the fury in her expression.

"So, did you two plan Valda's death together? Was it Tony's idea, or yours?"

Roger bolted up from the couch and glared into Jo's eyes. "How dare you?"

"How dare I? How dare I figure out that you've been lying to us this entire time about something that you never should have kept from us? The only reason why you wouldn't tell the truth is because you were involved."

"What are you talking about?" He took an aggressive step towards Jo, which prompted Eddy to move between them.

"Watch it," Eddy warned.

"I'm talking about the fact that Tony called you at almost the exact time of Valda's death. That's what I'm talking about. Tony, the man you stole the necklace with, called you before you ever called the police about your wife's death. So, why are you lying to us? Why are we here right now doing this sting operation when we have the murderer, at least one of them, right in front of us?"

"I didn't kill her! I didn't!" Roger nearly screamed. "You're wrong. You have no idea what you're talking about."

"Then tell me. Tell me why Tony called you. Don't lie to me and say you didn't speak to him because I have proof that the conversation lasted over three minutes. A lot can be said in three minutes, Roger."

"That's not what happened!" Roger groaned. "All right, fine, if you want to know the truth, yes I did talk to Tony. That's why I went home when I did."

"Why? What did Tony say?" Jo stared at him.

"He called to taunt me. He called to tell me that he was out of prison, that he had taken the necklace, and that I would pay the price, just like he had to."

"And you never thought to tell us any of this?"

"What does it matter?" Roger demanded. "I rushed home and Valda was dead. I knew Tony killed her and took the necklace. I still couldn't tell the police."

"Did he confess to killing Valda?" Jo stepped towards him. "Did he tell you that on the phone?"

"No, he just said he took the necklace. But when I got home she was dead. So obviously he killed her."

"Obviously you've been lying to us from the very beginning, Roger. I don't even know why I bothered to help you," Jo said.

"Don't get high and mighty with me." Roger scowled at her. "I told you it was Tony. You were too busy suspecting me to go after the person who really did it."

"But he didn't have the necklace, did he Roger? I don't know what to believe anymore!"

Eddy jumped up. "Take a breath, Jo. We'll know soon enough. Let's just let this play out and see where it ends up, all right?"

"All right." Jo sighed. She slouched down on the couch. It was a waiting game, and she didn't have the patience for it. She was angry at Roger for lying to her, angry at Drew for being involved, and angry that her past had resurfaced the way it had. She did her best to immerse herself in the television show. She stared at the screen. Her mind felt like it was turning to mush. She wasn't much for watching television. She much preferred to be in her garden. Outside she heard the loud sound of a motorcycle. All at once the hairs on the back of her neck stood up. She jumped to her feet.

"Eddy?" Jo said.

"Samantha just texted me. There's a motorcycle headed this way." A second later they heard the noise of the motorcycle at the end of the driveway. Jo walked towards the door. She listened closely. "Walt says no movement at Tony's and car is still in the driveway."

"But is Tony actually in the house? Maybe he had a motorcycle stashed somewhere?" Jo asked.

The sound of the motorcycle drew closer. Eddy fought with the keypad on his phone to text Walt.

"Auto correct." He muttered.

"Eddy!"

"He can't confirm that Tony is in the house."

"All right, game on. Everyone down and quiet." Jo crouched down, but she lingered by the door. The motorcycle engine cut off right in front of the villa. Jo's heart pounded. Could Tony have slipped out when Walt wasn't looking? Could it be Drew determined to get the necklace? Or was it another thief that was on their way to find it? There was a sharp knock on the door. Would a thief really knock?

"What should we do?" Roger whispered. Eddy and Jo exchanged a look.

"Open the door." Jo frowned. "He's coming in either way."

Roger grimaced. He crept towards the door. Jo moved right behind him, prepared to pounce. Eddy stepped up on the other side. Roger opened the door. Tony shoved his way right into the villa.

"So, you have the necklace? The necklace that belongs to me?" He screamed in Roger's face.

"You killed my wife!" Roger screamed back at him. "How could you kill an innocent woman?"

"Shut your mouth and give me my necklace!" Tony glared into his eyes. Jo moved to restrain him, but Eddy held up a hand to stop her.

"She was all I had in the world!" Roger lunged at Tony. He slammed his fist across Tony's face. Tony stumbled back, then lunged forward and tried to tackle Roger to the ground. Eddy moved to jump into the fray, but Tony landed his foot in Eddy's stomach which knocked him back several feet. Jo pounced onto Tony's back to try to pull him off Roger. As she struggled with him, Tony reached up and behind his body. He grabbed at her hair and neck. Jo gulped down air as he twisted around and managed to squeeze her neck. In the middle of all the chaos she realized she had put herself in an impossible position. Tony had his legs twisted through hers and his hand wrapped tight around the side of her throat. It was getting harder for her to breathe. All of a sudden his hand was gone, as were his legs, and Tony was thrown to the ground. Jo stumbled to her feet to see Drew with Tony pinned beneath his thick, black boot.

"Drew?" Jo stared at him with wide eyes.

"Stay down." Drew kept one foot on Tony's back. "Don't move!"

Jo swallowed hard. She knew that Drew was still a thief, but she was still disappointed. She knew that he had probably come for the necklace. He had probably just saved her life, but she wished he hadn't. She wished he'd stayed a memory.

"The necklace isn't here, Drew." Jo rubbed at her throat and eyed him warily.

"It was a setup?" Drew raised an eyebrow and smirked. "Something else you learned from me, hmm?" Jo met his eyes and didn't say a word. She wanted to say a million things, not the least of which was to accuse him of murder. He was there for a reason, and she knew that she was not it. "And you don't have it either, hmm?" He looked down at Tony. "It must be a terrible thing to know that that beautiful necklace, the very reason you were in prison for so long, still isn't yours to keep."

"Keep quiet!" Tony growled. He tried to get out from under Drew's boot, but Drew held him in place.

"The police are on their way." Eddy hung up his phone. Drew's eyes snapped towards him.

"Then I'll be going," Drew said.

"Wait just a second. Not so fast." Eddy moved in front of the door. "No one is going anywhere.

There's still a matter of a missing necklace."

"It's not missing, Tony has it." Jo glared at the man on the ground. "It's the only thing that makes sense. I guess he just thought it might be a good idea to come here and wipe out the last witness to his crime. He killed Valda, and was going to kill Roger next."

"That's not true!" Tony squirmed under Drew's shoe. "I'm here to look for the necklace."

"I know you had it!" Roger accused as he stood up from where he was hiding behind the couch. "You told me you had it."

"Okay fine, I did steal it. If you can call it stealing, since it was mine in the first place."

"You mean, you stole it in the first place." Eddy frowned.

"So, where is the necklace?" Drew applied pressure to Tony's back. "You must have it."

"I did have it, I did. Valda handed it right to me. She didn't even fight me."

"But you still murdered her?" Jo stared down at him with disgust.

"I did not!" Tony struggled to get free. "I didn't kill anyone! I just wanted the necklace. Why would I kill her?"

"If you didn't kill her, then who did?" Eddy threw his hands up with exasperation.

"Maybe someone else came looking for the necklace?" Tony lifted his head. "It's not like I'm the only one who wanted it. There were others who wanted it just as bad. Isn't that right, Drew?" Tony turned his head in an attempt to look up at him, but Drew increased the pressure of his shoe against the man's back.

"Stop trying to blame other people for your own actions. I had nothing to do with the missing necklace," Drew said.

"But that's why you're here isn't it? To get it back?" Tony said.

"Maybe. Or maybe I am here to make sure that my friend is safe." He looked at Jo and met her eyes. "Now, are you going to return the favor, Jo, or are you going to watch them haul me away in handcuffs?"

"Go, just go!" Jo lunged between Eddy and Drew to make sure that Drew had a clear path through the back door.

"Jo! Move out of the way!" Eddy tried to get past her, but Jo stood her ground until Drew was gone. Before Eddy could argue with Jo, a police officer burst through the front door of the villa. For a tense moment, Jo waited for Eddy to send him after Drew. Eddy stared hard at her, but he did not mention Drew.

"Officer, this man is involved in a murder and a theft." Eddy pointed at Tony who had just gotten to his feet.

"Theft of what?" The officer looked between all of them.

"A necklace." Roger frowned. Eddy sent a text to Walt saying he could take a break from the surveillance on Tony's place.

"Where's the necklace? Do you have it?" The officer looked at Tony.

"These people are crazy, I didn't steal anything."

"He doesn't have the necklace." Eddy attempted to explain. Jo tried to remain incognito.

"So, he broke into the house?" The officer made a note on his notepad.

"No, he didn't break in actually." Roger hung his head. "I let him in."

"So, you let him into the house and then he attacked you?" The officer made another note. Roger groaned and shook his head.

"No. I think, I might have been the one to attack him first."

"So, there is really no reason to arrest this man?" The officer raised an eyebrow. He looked over at Tony. "Do you want to press charges against this man for assault?"

Tony stared hard at Roger. Then he shook his head. "No officer. I'd just like to be on my way if that's all right with you."

"And you two?" The officer turned to look at Jo and Eddy. "Did you have a part in all of this?"

"Not exactly." Eddy frowned. Jo just shook her head. She could have told the officer about Tony threatening her, but in order to do that she would have to reveal that Drew was present and had fled before the police arrived, which would only complicate things. Besides all of that she was still scared of the police and wanted to avoid talking to them wherever possible.

"All right then. I think you should leave." He said to Tony. "The two of you need to stay away from each other. Understand?" He gestured between Roger and Tony.

"Yes sir." Tony nodded.

Eddy could not hold his tongue any longer. "Don't you think this should be looked into a little more?" He walked over to the officer. "A woman is dead."

"Uh." The officer skimmed through the information on his phone. "There is a suspicious death, but there is no confirmation of any foul play. I will pass on the information to the relevant people and see what they want to do. I don't know anything about this necklace that you're talking about, but if you want to make a theft report I'll need a description of the item. Do either of you want to do that?" He looked from Roger to Tony.

"No." Roger stood up.

"No." Tony shook his head.

"Then there is nothing else I can do here." The officer scrutinized Eddy. "You look familiar to me."

"You've probably seen me around the station." Eddy sighed. "I'm retired."

"Oh, I see." The officer smiled. "Still working the beat, huh?"

"Something like that." Eddy gritted his teeth.

"Well, it looks like this one is a non-issue. So, let's all agree to move on and have no further contact, hmm?" The officer looked at each person in turn. "I don't want to have to come out here again."

"You don't have to tell me twice." Tony moved past the officer and right out the door. The officer followed after him with a slight nod of his head. Jo pushed the door closed behind him.

"Unbelievable." Eddy shook his head.

"What did you expect?" Jo raised an eyebrow. "You should have discussed it with me before calling the police."

"Things got a little out of control, don't you think, Jo?" Eddy eyed her with annoyance.

"It seemed to me that Drew got them back under control."

"Drew? You mean the criminal that you encouraged to run away before the police could get here?"

"Eddy, I can explain."

"Is he the one who you caught breaking into Roger's house?" Jo glanced over at Roger and then back to Eddy. She didn't speak. "The one whose face you claimed not to see?" Eddy pressed.

"It's not important now, is it?" She met his eyes. "I just want to get this case solved."

"Well, that's not going to happen now, is it? Our main suspect wasn't even arrested by the police. It's clear that he didn't kill Valda, and that he doesn't have the necklace. There's nothing more that we can do here," Eddy said.

"No there's not because now that the police have been here no one else is going to show up to look for the necklace. The plan is blown, and we are no closer to knowing the truth than when we started."

"And that's my fault?" Eddy stared at her with widened eyes. "How can you truly believe that it is my fault when you obviously were very friendly with a criminal that has been involved in this crime possibly from the first moment?"

"What are you saying?" Jo stared at him.

"I'm saying that you have been protecting Drew from suspicion, when he is just as likely to be as guilty as Roger or Tony."

"I didn't do it!" Roger growled. "I'm standing right here you know. I didn't do it!"

"Shush!" Jo looked over at Roger with a sharp glare. "I don't think that Drew is capable of murder."

"But you don't get to decide that, Jo. He showed up here didn't he? Who is to say that he didn't go looking for that necklace after Tony took it, only to kill Valda when she caught him?"

Jo's heart dropped. She hadn't really thought of that. When Tony admitted to stealing the necklace, she thought that cleared Drew, but it didn't. Eddy was right. Drew could have murdered Valda. He could have also shown up at Roger's when he did with the intention of killing him.

"I'm sorry, Eddy." Jo looked down at her

hands. "I guess I didn't think it through far enough. Or maybe I just didn't want to think that he was involved. I mean, he did save us from Tony."

"Did he? Or did he just do that to solidify the idea of his innocence in your mind?"

Jo thought about it for a moment and then shook her head. "I don't know. I'm not sure."

"That's the problem. We have nothing. We have no evidence to point to anyone. We're going to have to let this one go, Jo."

"Seriously?"

"What about Valda?" Roger stepped in between them. "You're just going to give up?"

"It's not like you did much for her," Eddy snapped. "You could have told the police about the necklace and your suspicions about her death if you really wanted her death to be investigated properly. Now we've spent a lot of time and effort to untangle the mess you made, Roger, but it's still your mess. We couldn't even get Tony arrested because you couldn't admit to having the necklace in your possession at one time."

"Wait a minute. Wait a minute." Jo held up her hands. "If Tony doesn't have the necklace, then who has it?"

"Why are you back on that again?" Eddy narrowed his eyes.

"I think that we need to take a step back. We're missing something here." Jo shook her head.

"Yes, we're missing the fact that there is no way to solve this crime. I'm ready to get out of here."

"Wait a minute, you're going to leave me here alone, after leaking the fact that I have the necklace?" Roger grabbed onto Eddy's wrist. "You can't do that. They'll eat me alive."

"So, call the cops." Eddy shook Roger's hand free. "You committed the crime in the first place, Roger, maybe you should just turn yourself in and take your chances with prison."

"Eddy, please, we can't..."

"Don't, Jo." Eddy shook his head. "I'm going home." He stepped out of the villa and slammed the door closed behind him. Jo felt terrible because she knew she was the source of his frustration. He wasn't angry that they couldn't solve the crime, or even that Roger had stolen the necklace in the first place, but because she had protected Drew. She took a deep breath and looked over at Roger.

"Don't worry, I'll stay with you tonight and by tomorrow we'll have the rumor cleared up so that you won't be targeted."

"But what about Valda?" Roger frowned. "Someone should have to pay for what happened to my wife."

Jo nodded as she turned to look out the front window of the villa. "You're right, Roger. We just don't know who. You lying about so much, hasn't helped this investigation much."

"I know. I guess once you get used to lying, it's

just what you do."

Chapter Fifteen

Eddy burst into Walt's villa without even knocking. Walt jumped up and nearly spilled his cup of tea. He caught it before it could hit the floor and shatter.

"I can't believe her!"

"Who?" Walt stared at him.

"Jo! That's who." Eddy shook his head and balled his hands into fists. "You think you know someone."

"What are you talking about, where is Jo?"

"She's at Roger's villa."

"Wait a minute, are you saying you left her alone with a thief and potential murderer?" Walt stared at Eddy with disbelief. "How could you do that?"

"She's a grown woman and decided to stay on her own." Eddy shrugged. "Women's lib and all of that, right?"

"Eddy." Walt glared at him. "Stop trying to act big and tough, I know you better than that. What really happened?"

"What happened is that she lied to me, Walt. I thought we were past all of that."

"Lied about what?" Walt paused. "Oh, you found out about Drew?"

"You knew? Is everyone lying to me now?"

"I didn't exactly know. There's a lot of history there, Eddy. You can't blame her for doing what she thought was best."

"What if he was the one who murdered Valda, Walt?" Eddy frowned.

"All the more reason not to leave her alone." Walt picked up his coat. "I'm going over there. I'm going to let Samantha know to keep up the surveillance. Are you going to come with me or not?"

"Why should I if I don't know if I can trust her?"

"Maybe that isn't the problem, Eddy. Maybe the question you should be asking yourself, is, why doesn't she trust you?" Walt brushed past him. "At this point, I wonder if you would turn so easily against any of your friends. What are you really angry about, Eddy? The fact that she lied, or the fact that she still feels the need to hide things about herself from you?"

Eddy watched as Walt walked through the door. "Lock up behind you please." Walt closed the door. Eddy stood alone in the middle of Walt's living room. He didn't want Walt's logical nature to creep through his fury and force everything he said to make sense to him, but it did. He decided that he needed to go back to Roger's as well. If he wanted Jo to believe that she could trust him, he had to give her reason to.

***

Jo paced back and forth in front of the window. Her mind traveled from the past to the present. She wanted to be angry at Eddy. She wanted to be able to declare that he was dead wrong. But the truth was, he was right. She had given Drew far more benefit of the doubt than he deserved. If he was involved in the crime, if he was a suspect, she should have been honest every step of the way with Eddy. Instead she tried to protect Drew from the scrutiny of her friends, or maybe it was more about protecting herself and her past choices from their scrutiny. Either way she put the entire investigation at risk. Not that there was an investigation left to speak of now, anyway.

"Could you please sit down?" Roger looked over at her from the couch. "You're making me dizzy."

"Did you kill your wife, Roger?" Jo turned to face him.

"How many times do I have to answer that question?" He stared up at her. His glare and the tone of his voice bothered Jo to the point that she decided not to hold back any longer.

"Let me throw a scenario out there. Let's just say that you came home from the buffet, and you found Valda, only she was still alive. She was upset. She wanted to go to the police about the stolen necklace. She wanted to turn Tony in, have him arrested for the crime. You, never told her how you really got the necklace, did you Roger?"

Roger's eyes widened. "No."

"Right. So you come home, Valda's in a panic, she's got her phone out, she's dialing the emergency line. You try to get her to stop, to listen..."

"No." Roger shook his head.

"But she won't listen. She wants her necklace back. You try to get the phone from her."

"No I didn't," Roger whispered. "I didn't do any of that."

"She's getting irate, she doesn't understand why you are trying to stop her. She starts screaming, maybe cursing, threatening you!"

"No!" Roger stood up. "None of that happened!"

"Yes, you're angry. You're angry because Tony stole the necklace, and you're angry that your wife won't listen to you and wants to call the police. You just want her to keep quiet." Jo met his eyes and took a step towards him. "So what did you do? You picked up a muffin. You shoved it into her mouth, just to make her be quiet. That was all you were going to do. You just wanted her to be quiet long enough that you could figure out what to do." Jo paused for a moment and crossed her arms across her chest. "I think I'm right, Roger. You didn't mean to kill her you just wanted her to keep quiet. The lie you'd been living for so long was crashing down around you, and you knew that if Valda told the truth, you would be in prison for a very long time. You just wanted her to be quiet. That was all."

"No, no, no!" Roger turned away from her. Just as he did there was a knock on the door. Jo jumped at the sound. Roger gasped. "This is it. I'm going to die tonight. I deserve to die anyway." Tears streamed down his cheeks. Jo crept towards the door.

"Who's there?" Jo asked cautiously.

"It's me, Walt."

Jo jerked the door open and found Walt on the doorstep.

"What are you doing here?"

"I'm here to stay with you, to make sure that you're safe." Walt met her eyes through his thick glasses. Jo couldn't help but smile a little. She was about to thank him, when there was a crash. She spun around to see that Roger had barreled through the back door.

"He's bolting!" Jo started to run after him, but Walt grabbed her arm.

"What are you going to do if you catch him?"

"Walt! He's getting away!" Jo tried to pull away, but Walt was stronger than she expected.

"What are you going to do if you catch him?" Walt asked again. "Are you going to arrest him? Tie him up? What?"

"He killed his wife!"

"Did he actually admit that?" Walt raised an eyebrow.

Jo paused. Then she shook her head. "No, I guess he didn't. But I still think he did it. It's the best explanation I've come up with."

"It doesn't mean it's true and even if it is that doesn't mean you can prove it."

"So, you're going to be just like Eddy and say that this is all over? We have to give up?"

"No." Eddy stepped through the door behind Walt. "No, that's not what we're going to do."

"Eddy?" Walt looked over at him and smiled. "I'm glad you're here."

"I'm sorry for earlier, Jo. You know me and my temper." Eddy rolled his eyes.

Jo sighed with relief. Only moments before she had felt completely alone, but here were her friends, ready to help.

"Roger took off." She pointed to the open back

door. "I was trying to get him to confess to killing Valda after Tony took the necklace."

"Do you believe that's what really happened?" Eddy closed the door behind him.

"I honestly don't know what to think anymore. I mean the timeline doesn't fit with Roger being the murderer." Jo shook her head. "Even if Tony took the necklace, he was a thief, not a murderer."

"You don't know that. He had decades in prison to plan his revenge on Roger," Eddy said. "Maybe he found it too hard to have the self-control to only take the necklace from Valda without causing her any harm."

"I find it hard to believe that Valda would give it up without a fight." Jo shook her head. "It's all too confusing. None of this is adding up. Something is still missing."

"Well, we're not going to find out anything else standing here."

"Do you think it's safe to leave?" Jo frowned.

"What if Roger comes back?"

"Roger made the choice to take off." Walt crossed his arms. "He's on his own now."

"All right." Jo nodded. "But just in case." She jotted down her phone number on a piece of paper and stuck it to the refrigerator.

"Do you think that's wise? Now if someone breaks in they'll have your number." Eddy frowned.

"Trust me, if they wanted it, they would already have it." Jo walked past the two men and out of the villa.

"Jo, let me walk you home." Walt stepped up beside her.

"No, thank you. I'm going to walk a bit and try to clear my mind."

"Are you sure?" Eddy frowned.

"I appreciate your concern, I really do. But I need some space. Okay?" She looked from Walt to Eddy. "Why don't you check in with Samantha and see if she needs any help putting out the fires we started."

"Jo, what about Drew?" Eddy reached for her arm. "Just because he protected you this time, that doesn't mean that you can trust him."

"I know that, Eddy." She gently pulled her arm away from him. "I don't trust him at all. I'm glad that he was here today, but the fact that he was here today is even more reason for me not to trust him. But I think that the police turning up today would have spooked him enough to leave me alone. Drew is not going to risk going to prison for any reason."

"Don't forget that Tony is out there, too. He's probably feeling pretty cocky about the fact that he got away with what he did today." Walt sighed. "But if you insist on walking alone, there's nothing that can be done."

"I do insist." Jo smiled at them both. "I am capable of taking care of myself, I promise."

"But you don't have to do everything alone."

Eddy met her eyes. "Call us if you have any trouble."

"I will."

Jo walked away from the pair with a warm sensation in her cheeks. It meant a lot to her that they were both so ready to protect her, even if she didn't feel as if she needed protection.

Jo wandered the streets for some time. She wasn't really looking for anything in particular, she just wanted to be outside in the open air. After confronting Roger multiple times she was beginning to believe that he was not guilty. He didn't crumble or confess. Maybe when he seemed a bit cold about his wife's death soon after she passed away it was because he was in shock. But now he seemed genuinely distressed by his wife's murder. But he was also the most likely person to have the necklace. Tony showed up, even Drew showed up, to look for the necklace. That meant that if their theory was correct neither of them had it.

Jo pulled out her phone to check in with Samantha to see if she had dug up any new leads. When she did she realized she still had the phone on silent from her search through Roger's villa. She had missed three calls from Roger. There was a voicemail as well. Jo turned her phone off silent and then she dialed in to listen to the voicemail. Roger's voice was high and frightened.

"Jo, someone is here I know it. Someone is looking in the windows. How could you leave? Where are you? Why did you make me a target? Please send someone to help me!"

Jo's heart stopped for a second, then began to race. She dialed Roger's number. The phone rang then went to voicemail. She broke into a sprint towards Roger's house. When she reached it, the windows were dark. There was no sign that anyone was inside. Jo called Roger's number again. Again the phone went to voicemail. She tried the doorknob. It wasn't locked. When the voicemail beeped she began to leave him a message.

"Roger, I'm at your place to check on you now."

Chapter Sixteen

Jo pushed her way through the door of Roger's villa and stepped into chaos. The entire pristine living room that Valda paid so much attention to decorating was destroyed. Furniture was overturned, paintings were ripped off the wall, even the silverware drawer had been emptied onto the kitchen floor. There didn't appear to be anyone in the villa. Jo's first thought was that someone must have abducted Roger. Then she heard a light rustling from the hallway.

Jo pulled out her phone and sent a text to Eddy to let him know that she needed help. Then she crept carefully down the hallway. If someone had done so much damage to the house and its contents, what might they have done to Roger? She made her way to the back bedroom. She could hear more subtle sounds of movement. Though she listened close she did not hear any voices or groans. The bedroom door was partway open. She was tempted to push it all the way open, but she had no idea what she would be walking into. Was Roger alone in there? Was someone else in there with a gun?

Just when she worked up the nerve to push the door open, her cell phone chirped. It was an announcement that she had received a text message. She could have kicked herself for not turning her ringer off after sending the text to Eddy. She knew that now whoever was in the bedroom knew that she was there, right there, outside the door. Her heart raced as she placed her fingertips against the smooth surface of the wooden door.

"Roger? I'm coming inside." She pushed on the door and then jumped back, just in case whoever was inside decided to fire. She was met with only silence. Slowly she poked her head around the corner of the doorway. In the middle of the room strapped to a wooden chair was Roger. He had tape over his mouth, but his eyes were wide open. They looked towards the closet.

Jo's heart pounded as she moved silently towards the closet. Her hand shook as she picked up a lamp from the bedside table.

She opened the closet door, with the lamp in her hand, ready to attack. Tony lunged out at her in the same moment that she swung the lamp forward. It connected with his head and shattered into pieces. Tony groaned and sank to his knees.

"Ow, you didn't have to do that!"

Jo grabbed the gun from Tony's hand. "And you didn't have to hide in a closet with a gun waiting for the chance to shoot me."

"Well, I didn't know what else to do!" Tony stood up slowly, stumbled out of the closet and sat down on the edge of the bed. Jo tucked the gun into the back of her pants and walked over to Roger to untie him. As she bent down to untie his feet, Tony jumped up and snatched the gun from her waistband. Jo spun around so fast that she almost lost her balance. She leaned heavily on Roger's knee to catch herself.

"Tony!" Jo shouted.

He pointed the gun at her. "Get away from him, back away." Tony gestured with the gun.

"Tony, I let you live, now this is how you're going to repay me?" Jo said.

Jo moved carefully to the side. She kept her eyes fixated on the gun. At any moment Tony might eliminate all of his problems, that meant her and Roger.

"Get down." Tony pointed to the corner of the room. "Don't move a muscle."

"I'm not moving. Just take it easy, Tony." Jo tried to meet his eyes, but he already looked back at Roger.

"Now, you're going to tell me where that necklace is. I know you stole it back from me." He reached out and ripped the duct tape off Roger's mouth in one swift movement. Roger let out a shriek.

"I didn't," Roger shouted. "I didn't take the necklace. I hope I never see that thing again. It wasn't worth it when I stole it. It's given me nothing but problems ever since."

"Why do you continue to lie to me?" Tony shook his head. "If you would just tell me what I need to know, all of this will be over."

"You'll just kill me, like you killed Valda."

"You can't prove that."

Jo froze. Those words sent a chill down her spine. It was true that they couldn't prove that Tony killed Valda, but that wasn't a denial of guilt.

"Please, Tony haven't you done enough to me? Haven't I paid enough?" Roger gasped.

"I don't know, Roger, have you spent years of your life locked behind bars while your partner in crime is completely free to do whatever they please? You are angry at me about losing your wife, but I never even had the chance to have one!"

Jo's heart jumped into her throat. The amount of venom in Tony's voice made her think that she and Roger were not going to get out of the situation alive.

"Tony, stop. Think about what you're doing. You're never going to get out of this. You're going to go back to prison or worse. Right now you have the chance to walk away," Jo said.

Jo's phone chimed again. Then again, several times, rapidly.

"Who is that? Who is contacting you?" Tony glared at her.

"It's nothing, just a friend, no one important."

"Did you tell someone that you were here?" Tony scowled. "Are you setting me up again?"

"No one knows." Jo clutched her phone tightly. "Maybe someone is looking for me."

"Well, they better not find you or they're going to be in a world of trouble, too." Tony reached out and snatched the phone from her hand. He flipped it over and looked at the screen. Whatever was on the screen made his eyes widen. He dropped the phone to the floor and released the safety on his gun. "All right, Roger, last chance to come clean. Trust me, you'd rather be alive. There's nothing in this world worth dying for."

"I don't have it." Roger closed his eyes. "I went looking for it to steal it back, but I couldn't find it."

"I looked, too." Jo edged the phone closer to her with the tip of her toe. She tried to get Tony's attention off Roger before he could pull the trigger. "I didn't find anything. I thought it was in the curtain rod..."

"It was!" Tony turned the gun on her. "You do have it!"

"I don't!" Jo managed to get a glimpse of the text on her phone.

Be careful. The medical examiner flagged Valda's death as a homicide. An official investigation has been started. It might spook the murderer.

Jo grimaced. Thanks a lot, Eddy, she thought to herself. Tony was definitely spooked. "That's it, there's no more time to argue. One of you is going to tell me the truth right this second or you're both going to die." Tony raised the gun and pointed it at Jo. "You can be the first, since you can't seem to mind your own business." Jo's eyes widened. She knew that she was out of excuses. Drew had saved her once, would he be able to do it again? Tony had a gun. There was no escape.

Just then Samantha burst through the bedroom door with a flurry of swinging arms and shouting. Jo stared at her, perplexed. Samantha continued to swing her arms and shout. Tony stared at her as well with his mouth half open. Suddenly, Eddy jumped through the window behind them. In the same moment that Eddy's feet struck the floor with a loud thump Walt burst through the door from behind Samantha and tackled Tony to the floor. Eddy piled on top of Walt and wrenched the gun out of Tony's hand. In the middle of it all Roger struggled to get out of his chair, while Jo continued to only stare with shock. She blinked when Samantha finally stopped shouting.

"What was that?" Jo stepped back as Eddy wrestled with Tony until he had him locked into a set of zip ties.

"You're alive aren't you?" Samantha grinned.

"Good point." Jo shook her head. "You guys managed to arrive right on time."

"Are you okay?" Walt looked over at her, his brows knitted with concern.

"I'm okay." She nodded. "It looks like we have our murderer here. Don't we, Tony?"

Tony rested his head against the floor and sighed. "All right. It was an accident, but I guess it doesn't matter now, does it?"

"Yes, it matters," Roger whispered. "It matters why my wife had to die, when all you had to do was ask me for the necklace."

"Like you would have given it to me." Tony

twisted his head to glare at him.

"If you had given me a choice between Valda and the necklace, yes I absolutely would have given it to you. She stayed with me even when I had nothing."

"It's easy for you to say that now, but that's not what would have happened and you know it."

"I guess we'll never know." Jo crossed her arms. "Because Valda is dead. You killed her."

"It was an accident." He groaned. "I just wanted her to be quiet. When I told her that Roger was a thief, that her necklace was stolen, she kept shouting at me that it wasn't possible, that I was a liar. Then when I tried to take the necklace from her, she ran for the couch and screamed. I tried to catch her, but she got away. She was running for the door and I grabbed a pillow." He rested his forehead against the floor. "I just needed her to stop. I needed her to slow down before she drew too much attention. I put the pillow over her face and held it there until she was quiet. But then…"

"It was too late." Eddy frowned.

"I just wanted her to stop. I just wanted the necklace. I never meant to kill her." He shook his head. "If only she had just kept quiet, and given me what I asked for."

"It was not her fault!" Roger shouted. "You can't blame her for her own murder."

"It wasn't murder, it was an accident," Tony said.

"Well, I guess we'll have to let the police decide that. I am calling them right now, okay Jo?" Eddy met her eyes.

"Yes, please." She nodded.

"We all heard your confession, Tony. We all know you tied Roger up and held a gun on Jo. You are not getting out of this one," Eddy said.

"But I don't have the necklace."

"No one cares about the necklace." Jo crouched down beside him. "We care about Valda. Now her death will not go unnoticed or unpunished."

As they waited for the police to arrive Jo felt a sense of peace wash over her. Maybe they hadn't solved the entire crime, the necklace was still missing, but Tony was going to pay for Valda's murder. When the officer arrived, Jo recognized him from the last time Eddy called the police. He looked from Roger tied up in the chair, to Tony zip tied on the floor.

"I'm assuming that there is a very good explanation for this?" He looked from Eddy to Jo.

"Officer, this man murdered this man's wife." Eddy pointed from Tony to Roger. "He came here tonight to murder him, and my friend, Jo."

"Murder him?" the officer asked.

"I only killed her because he took the necklace I stole! I never meant it." Tony thrashed on the ground. "He deserves to be in prison, he's a thief!"

"Sir, are you aware that you are confessing to murder?" The officer stared down at him.

"Yes. Yes, I confess to it all. It was an accident,

but what do I care? I've lived most of my life in prison, I'm going back either way. But this time, I'm not going back alone. You're going to pay the price right along beside me, Clem!"

Roger was pale as the officer called for back-up. He didn't speak a word. Jo stood quietly as she tried to keep the officer's attention off her. Walt touched Jo's shoulder lightly.

"You did good, Jo. You didn't give up."

"I guess." Jo frowned. "But we still have no idea where the necklace is."

"One of them must have it. I'm sure some good old fashioned police interrogation will get to the bottom of it all." Eddy winked at her.

"I hope so," Jo said.

Samantha grabbed Jo's hand. "I'd love to write an article about this, what do you think?"

"I think it's better that you don't." Jo frowned. "If people know that the necklace is missing, Sage Gardens will experience a very strange kind of gold rush."

"Ah, good point." Samantha nodded. "It's a shame, it would have been a great article."

"Maybe one day, Samantha, if the necklace is ever found."

"All right, everyone, I'm going to need statements." The officer took a deep breath and flipped open his notepad.

Chapter Seventeen

It was dark by the time Jo began to walk back to her villa. For the first time she didn't expect anyone to be hiding in the bushes or following her. Yet as she approached her street, she felt on edge yet again. She felt like someone was following her.

"Not again." She reached up and rubbed the back of her neck. "This is getting ridiculous."

She paused beneath one of the street lights and looked all around her. Suddenly there was a flash of a figure, just a shadow, that swung from the roof of one villa to the roof of another. When the figure landed it jumped down just as swiftly from that roof and disappeared behind a tall bush. Jo stared hard at the bush. She knew that if she stepped any closer she would be putting herself at risk, but if she stayed right where she was she would risk never getting to find out who was following her. She walked away from the street that led to her villa and towards the bush. When she reached the bush she found nothing. There was no one hidden behind it. She shook her head. Had it been her imagination? An illusion created by the light? Perhaps a cloud passed over the moon at just the right moment. She started to turn back towards her street.

As she did she caught sight of the figure again. It disappeared just as fast down her street. Jo broke into a run in an attempt to catch up to the person, but there was no one to chase. Whoever it was, was gone, yet again. Frustrated, she stalked towards her villa and instead of going straight in she walked past it and into her garden. Though it was dark and the beauty of it was dulled by the lack of light, it still comforted her. It soothed her nerves enough that she could let go of the memory of the figure. She took a deep breath of the air that was thick with the smell of soil and willed her body to relax. A lot had happened over the past few days. Old memories surfaced and new memories were made.

Once Jo was calm again she stepped into her villa through the back door. She tossed her things on the kitchen counter and headed down the hallway. She walked into her bedroom ready to collapse. She was still frustrated over Drew's ability to evade her. She knew that she had lost the necklace once and for all. It would never be returned to the family it was originally stolen from, and Valda's death, though now solved, would still not be completely resolved.

As Jo sat down at the foot of her bed she felt some relief. At least Tony was back behind bars where he belonged. She stretched out on the bed, but when she laid her head on her pillow it hit something hard. She jumped up and turned to see the 'Rose Diamond' necklace stretched out across her pillow. Pinned beneath it was a short note.

It's finally yours.

Love always,

Drew

She stared at the note and the necklace with absolute disbelief. Drew stole the necklace, just to give it to her? Her heart began to race, not only because of old feelings, but because she would be able to return the necklace to its rightful owners.

Jo picked up the necklace and studied it intently. All at once she knew what had happened. Drew followed her to Tony's house. While she was outside with Roger threatening to shoot her he broke in through the front door, just as he had taught her, and took the necklace from the curtain rod before she even had the chance to look for it. That was why the door was left open. Then he showed up to pretend to take the bait, as he recognized her plan as his own. The entire time he had the necklace. He was still a thief, and he would always be a thief, but he was not a murderer. That gave Jo quite a bit of comfort.

Drew had given her a treasure, but the real treasure she discovered, was the love and loyalty of her friends. She picked up her phone to call Samantha. She would have an article to write after all.

The End

More Cozy Mysteries by Cindy Bell

Sage Gardens Cozy Mysteries

Birthdays Can Be Deadly

Money Can Be Deadly

Trust Can Be Deadly

Ties Can Be Deadly

Rocks Can Be Deadly

Chocolate Centered Cozy Mysteries

The Sweet Smell of Murder

A Deadly Delicious Delivery

Dune House Cozy Mysteries

Seaside Secrets

Boats and Bad Guys

Treasured History

Hidden Hideaways

Dodgy Dealings

Suspects and Surprises

Heavenly Highland Inn Cozy Mysteries

Murdering the Roses

Dead in the Daisies

Killing the Carnations

Drowning the Daffodils

Suffocating the Sunflowers

Books, Bullets and Blooms

A Deadly serious Gardening Contest

A Bridal Bouquet and a Body

Wendy the Wedding Planner Cozy Mysteries

Matrimony, Money and Murder

Chefs, Ceremonies and Crimes

Knives and Nuptials

Mice, Marriage and Murder

Bekki the Beautician Cozy Mysteries

Hairspray and Homicide

A Dyed Blonde and a Dead Body

Mascara and Murder

Pageant and Poison

Conditioner and a Corpse

Mistletoe, Makeup and Murder

Hairpin, Hair Dryer and Homicide

Blush, a Bride and a Body

Shampoo and a Stiff

Cosmetics, a Cruise and a Killer

Lipstick, a Long Iron and Lifeless

Camping, Concealer and Criminals

Treated and Dyed

Printed in Great Britain
by Amazon